I'll Always Love You Paperback
INCLUDES BONUS NOVELLA
Ground Rules
Copyright © 2023 Lorhainne Ekelund
Editor: Talia Leduc

All rights reserved.
ISBN-13: 978-1998775491

Give feedback on the book at:
lorhainneeckhart@hotmail.com

Twitter: @LEckhart
Facebook: AuthorLorhainneEckhart

Printed in the U.S.A

I'll Always Love You

THE FRIESSENS
BOOK NINETEEN

LORHAINNE ECKHART

The Friessen Family Series
Reading order:

The Outsider Series

The Forgotten Child
A Baby And A Wedding
Fallen Hero
The Awakening
Secrets
Runaway
Overdue
The Unexpected Storm
The Wedding

The Friessens: A New Beginning

The Deadline
The Price to Love
A Different Kind of Love
A Vow of Love, A Friessen Family Christmas

The Friessens

The Friessen Family

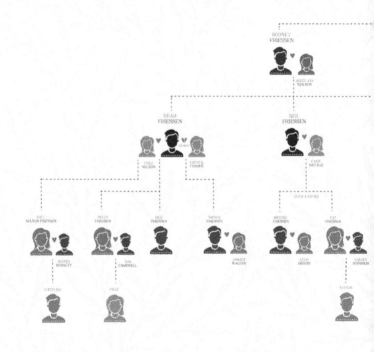

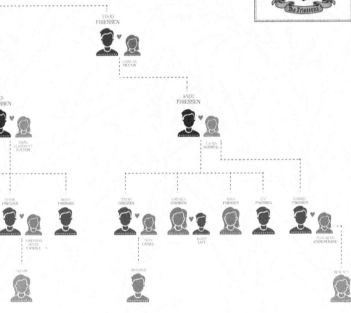

The Friessens

THE ENTIRE FRIESSEN FAMILY
ANDY & LAURA
RED & DIANA
NEIL & CANDY
BRAD & EMILY
KATY & STEVEN
KATY & STEVEN

The Friessens

LEAVE THE LIGHT ON
IN THE MOMENT
IN THE FAMILY
IN THE SILENCE
IN THE STARS
IN THE CHARM
UNEXPECTED CONSEQUENCES

KATY & STEVEN
BECKY & TOM
THE ENTIRE FRIESSEN FAMILY
CAT & XANDER
DANNY & EVIE
CHRIS & LIL
CHRIS & LIL

The Friessens

IT WAS ALWAYS YOU
THE FIRST TIME I SAW YOU
WELCOME TO MY ARMS
WELCOME TO BOSTON
I'LL ALWAYS LOVE YOU
GROUND RULES
A REASON TO BREATHE
YOU ARE MY EVERYTHING
ANYTHING FOR YOU
THE HOMECOMING

KATY & STEVEN
GABRIEL & ELIZABETH
CHELSEA & ALARIC
PAYT & MORGAN
JEREMY
JEREMY & TIFFY
TREVOR & JASMINE
MICHAEL & ANGIE
THE ENTIRE FRIESSEN FAMILY

I'll Always Love You

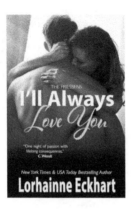

When a one-night stand from years ago comes back to town, Jeremy meets the son he never knew he had...

She's his best friend's sister.

After one night together Tiffy Cahill up and leaves town only to return three years later with a secret that could have Jeremy Friessen wishing she had never returned.

> "One night of passion with lifelong consequences. A rollercoaster of emotions and riveting love story." *(C. Wendt, Reviewer)*

But what Jeremy doesn't know is why she left, whatever her secret is--whatever her reason was for disappearing, Jeremy is determined to find out everything, and when he does he may wish he'd never found her.

Ground Rules
Bonus Novella

With their wedding less than a week away, Jeremy and Tiffy discover they're not on the same page when it comes to raising their son and dealing with the challenges that come their way. In true Friessen fashion, when Jeremy tries to establish ground rules, he soon learns that Tiffy isn't the kind of woman anyone can tell what to do, and his strong personality could have her calling off the wedding and walking the other way.

CHAPTER

One

"You almost finished up there?"

Jeremy heard the scratchy voice of Dot, short for Dorothy, who was the owner of Dot's Stop, the hardware store just outside the city center of Columbia Falls. Jeremy closed up the box of plastic PVC pipes from where he was crouched in the dusty attic, doing inventory the old-school way, with a clipboard and pencil, because Dot was a believer that going digital was a recipe for impending disaster. No matter how much Jeremy tried to convince her of the efficiency and ease, not to mention the better use of his time, she wouldn't budge. If everything were digitally recorded, at her fingertips, so she knew exactly what she had, he'd never be stuck in a too-small attic again.

"Yeah, just..." He stood up and banged his head on the sloped attic ceiling. "Ah, shit!" he yelled and dropped the clipboard. For a second, he thought he saw stars as he took in the century-old attic where all the extra stock was stored—dusty, dark, damp. It was a crime, in his mind.

"You hit your head again, Jer?" Her deep laugh was

raspy and almost sounded like a man's as he made his way to the square hole in the floor where the wooden ladder hung down. Dot was in a red and white shirt that resembled a bowling league uniform, in her fifties, with long thick white hair that did nothing for her five-foot-five plump stature. She was still using the nickname she'd bestowed on him even after he'd reminded her a dozen or so times that he preferred Jeremy. He thought, though, it was her twisted sense of humor, and the fact was that she loved pushing his buttons. It was evident by the expression on her face as she stared up at him now.

"It would be great if there was an actual storage room instead of a spot that only fits a kid. Speaking of which, it would be better if you sent up Ruth or Cady, who are half my size…" He slipped his sneakered foot down on the rail of the ladder, gripping the clipboard, and climbed down. He still couldn't believe he'd squeezed all the boxes of stock through into the attic, and he knew he was the one who'd have to haul each box down, not Dot or Ruth or Cady.

She said nothing as he stood in front of her, wiping the dust off his favorite Cubs T-shirt and his deep blue wranglers. He towered over Dot, feeling as if he'd breathed half the dust into his lungs, and she held out her hand for the clipboard. "Stop your complaining, would you?" she said. "Ruth and Cady don't have your brute strength to move the boxes. Besides, I needed the count today, and they're not working. You are."

He slapped the clipboard in her hand. She never pulled her amber eyes from him, and then she dragged her gaze down, sweeping over him from head to toe and all the way back up, landing on his face before a slow easy smile touched her lips.

"You sure are a looker, there, Jer, just like your daddy."

She made a sound of appreciation, the kind that totally creeped him out, even though he knew she was married with four grown kids. Something about that cougar type of teasing made him feel like prey. Dot then turned away and started walking back to the front of the store, where she slipped behind the counter. The small cluttered shop seemed to sell just about anything and everything, and even though he'd worked there for just over two years, he still didn't know where everything was. He wanted to remind Dot to stop calling him Jer, but he knew it would be wasted breath.

"Truth be told," Dot said, "if you really want to know, Cady actually volunteered to come in on her day off to help with the inventory." She flicked her gaze up to him as he stopped just short of where she lingered behind the counter, scribbling something down before she flicked the pen and then glanced up to him. "To help you out," she added with effect.

It took him a second to understand her meaning. "You mean…"

He didn't finish as another slow smile touched Dot's lips. Her eyes simmered with that teasing heat that had him wanting to take another step back. "Come on, Jer," she said. "You have to know the girls here have the hots for you. The customers, too, who come in and wait for you and only you to wait on them. Add in the fact that every time you go up and down that ladder, every girl around is watching you, the way you move all those heavy boxes. Cady's had eyes for you since the day you started working here over two years ago. She's been drooling over you ever since. Haven't you figured that out? You just have to look her way, toss the poor girl a crumb, and the girl is ready and willing to do anything just to be around you, with you, talking to you. Seriously, can't believe you don't see it. Told her to knock it off, but it's as if you've cast this spell over her. Then there's Ruth, the way she watches you when she thinks you're not looking, all dreamy-like."

Again, he just stared at Dot, not sure what expression was on his face as he pictured dark-eyed Cady, who wore glasses and was a senior in high school, he thought. Then there was Ruth, thin, young, with two little ones running around. Her husband was a roughneck, always out on the rigs, never home, and he didn't like the picture that thought painted. Dot had to be wrong.

"Face it, Jer," she said. "You're cursed by your father's good looks, so much so that every red-blooded and breathing woman in a one-hundred-mile radius would likely follow you home if they thought you'd give them the time of day. And don't forget that arrogance and that badass attitude, the fact you never go with the crowd but always walk your own way. You're the kind of strong-minded male women love. It sets you apart from every average Joe out there. Women love that." She tapped the counter, and he couldn't come up with a reasonable thing to say as he took in the empty store, the locked door, and the clock above her, which was sitting at ten past seven. Jeremy was unsettled by the image she'd placed in his head.

He pulled in a breath, wondering whether someone was going to jump out and tell him this was all a big joke. "I think you're trying to mess with me, Dot," he said.

She just rolled her eyes. "Try looking in a mirror, and if that doesn't work, ask your girlfriend." She lifted her hand in a wave as she stepped around the counter.

"I don't have a girlfriend," he called out, but she was already walking to the locked front door and flicking the deadbolt to pull it open. A relationship was the kind of commitment he really wasn't into. Sex was sex, but commitment was something else.

"Go home, Romeo," Dot called out over her shoulder.

Jeremy pulled out the keys to his F150 from his front pocket and started to the door. He shook his head at Dot and her peculiar personality as he stepped out onto the concrete sidewalk beside her, taking in his pickup across the half-empty parking lot, which they shared with the bingo hall, an old-time record store, and a sandwich shop.

"Hey, Jer, for the record," Dot said, "all that teasing and stuff is just that: teasing. I like you a lot. Seriously, you're a good guy even though you are easy on the eyes and a player. But here's some advice that you should take to heart. Find yourself a girl, a nice one, and leave that game-playing behind."

He took in Dot, trying to figure out where all this was coming from. "Thanks, but I like my single unattached life the way it is," he replied. The fact was, he didn't answer to anyone.

She shook her head and adjusted her big bulky purse over her shoulder as she locked the door. "Oh, there likely isn't a guy around who hasn't said that, and I bet your father said it, too, from the looks of him. But look at your parents, your family. You think your father is saying he wishes he had a simple, unencumbered, unattached life? I guarantee you he wouldn't trade you all for anything. We all see the way your parents are together, the way they look at each other when the other isn't looking. It's that kind of deep love that everyone wants but not everyone has. At the same time, women have been throwing themselves at good-looking men's feet since the beginning of time, and you not noticing isn't anything new."

"Dot, you're exaggerating," Jeremy said, but then, he also knew he'd never had to talk a woman into bed, into anything. He wasn't sure now why that bothered him, but it did, the way she made him seem almost…shallow. Then there were his parents, their life, their marriage—but he wasn't ready to be tied to anyone.

"Jer, I'm not," she said. "Listen up. There's worse things, and besides, you have a lot of other great qualities, too. You're reliable, a hard worker, and…" She tossed him the keys, which he caught as she started out to the parking lot. "And now you're in charge."

"What? No, wait!" He watched as she lifted her hand, walking over to her silver Dodge Ram four by four. "I'm not in charge," he said. "There's no way. I have commitments, college." He thought of the business course he'd finally agreed to take, how he'd compromised with his father instead of picking some Ivy League university for a degree he wasn't interested in. "And I'm only part-time."

"Just pop in when you can during the day," she said. "Ruth and Cady are there. You'll do fine, and besides, I trust you. I'm gone only two weeks. Just handle any problems and do everything I do." She climbed into her truck, and he just stood there with the keys. He didn't have a clue what Dot really did other than drink coffee, talk to customers, and tell all her employees what to do. Not only was he weirded out by what she'd said about Cady and Ruth loving him from afar, but he didn't like the idea that he suddenly had to be their boss.

He climbed into his truck and dumped his cell phone and wallet onto the center console, then pulled out of the lot and turned left instead of right, going into town. His phone beeped, and he lifted it, taking in the text as he stopped at a set of lights about three blocks from where his brother Gabriel lived. The text was from his best friend, Alex.

Party tonight at Kurts, got the keg!!

His thumb hovered over the reply when he heard a car honk. Seeing the light was green, he pressed the gas and started through the intersection.

It was then he spotted Alex's sister, Tiffy Cahill, in the oncoming traffic, behind the wheel of a beige older-model Volvo. Dark hair, gorgeous, and the image hit him from so long ago—how his hands had enjoyed the feel of her skin, her body, the night they'd spent together. It had been two, maybe three years ago, and her car was beside him as she passed.

She took him in, and he lifted his hand in a wave, thinking it'd be great to hook up, have some fun with her again, even though he shouldn't. But she pulled her gaze away as if she didn't have a clue who he was. *Like, what the hell?*

He kept driving and glanced in the rear-view mirror until he couldn't see her car anymore. His best friend's sister, one of the hottest nights of sex he'd ever had. Unforgettable. The memory alone stirred his interest, his desire. It wasn't smart on his part, considering guys never went after their friends' sisters if they wanted to stay out of the ER. He should put her out of his mind, never think of her that way again, never think about the touch, the kiss, how she tasted and felt, and the fun they'd had under the moon by the lake in the middle of summer.

Not long after that magical summer night, he realized now, Tiffy Cahill had all but disappeared.

CHAPTER

Two

He took in the gleaming white of his brother's kitchen, all high-end appliances with a huge granite center island. The home had an open concept, and he could see the living and dining room, the showpiece of the modest bungalow Gabriel had purchased as a fixer-upper. A can of what he thought was soda slid across the island to him.

"Uh…ginger ale? You couldn't come up with anything stronger?" Jeremy said as he cracked the can. He took a swallow, wishing for a beer, but that would come later, at Kurt's.

"You know I don't drink, and you're lucky there's even soda in the house," Gabriel said. "It's Elizabeth's. Also, let me remind you as your older and much wiser big brother that you're only nineteen, and it wouldn't go over well for you to be pulled over for any reason. In fact, Dad would likely kill me." Gabriel gestured to a plate of fish and left-overs from dinner on the counter.

Jeremy could hear Elizabeth and her cute little girl, Shaunty, from down the hall. He lifted his hand. "No, it's fine. Had a sandwich earlier on my break." He kind of wanted to save room for beer, and then he'd likely crash at Alex's, because he planned on having fun. Then there was Tiffy.

"So what gives?" Gabriel said. "It's not like you to just stop in like this, although it's great to see you. Seems you've got something on your mind."

Just then, Elizabeth walked in, and Shaunty scooted out the bar stool at the island beside Jeremy and climbed up. She was freshly bathed and in a cute pair of pajamas. Her curly dark hair was still damp, and she smiled brightly at him.

"There's ice cream, strawberry swirl," she said. "Do you want some? I'm having some, too. It's my favorite." She was so damn cute, and Jeremy took in Elizabeth in his brother's arms as she opened the fridge freezer. They seemed to be sharing a moment.

"Nope, I'll let you have it all, but thanks, though, kid."

She made a face, and he knew she was about to say something. "You know, I'm not a little kid," she said. "I'm six."

"Oops, my mistake, Miss Shaunty," he added, which had her giggling.

"You sure we can't tempt you, Jeremy?" Elizabeth said as she lifted the lid of the carton and scooped out the ice cream into two bowls. Gabriel was now leaning behind Elizabeth, his hands skimming her waist, her hips, as he kissed her neck, and they swayed together. It was almost embarrassing, at times, to be in a room with them.

"No, none for me." He lifted his hand just as Gabriel stepped around Elizabeth and looked at him intently. He realized everyone was staring at him, waiting for him to say something, he thought.

"Although I love the visits from you, I realize I'm not

Chelsea," Gabriel said. "It must be kind of hard not having her to bounce any ideas off since she up and left with Ric to Boston. So for you to just drop in like this, I'm thinking it must be something."

Jeremy took in the expression now on Elizabeth's face, in her dark eyes, as if she realized she'd just walked in on something. "Oh, it's just been a weird day, is all," Jeremy said. "Dot's suddenly put me in charge of the store, as she's decided to take off for a bit on holidays, and that was after she dropped a little bomb on me that two of my coworkers have been doing that 'love from afar' thing and following me around with puppy-dog eyes. At first I thought she was messing with me, which is what she does, but not this time. Now I'm supposed to go in and suddenly be in charge of them, knowing all this, and…" He lifted his hands, taking in the exchange between Elizabeth and Gabriel as she slid a bowl of ice cream in front of Shaunty, who was also watching him with interest and far too much amusement at his predicament for a kid her age. He really did miss Chelsea, and she hadn't returned his call from yesterday. Apparently moving away to Boston with Ric meant his twin sister was no longer as available for him.

"Girls like you," Shaunty said, staring up at him with dark eyes that reached inside him. She was the kind of kid, he thought, who could see the best in everyone. "Just be nice to them."

He didn't miss the smile Gabriel tried to hide. Shaunty had snuck in and grabbed a piece of his heart. She'd done that to all of them long ago.

"She's right. Great advice, Shaunty," Gabriel added.

Jeremy took in Elizabeth's brilliant smile as she dipped her spoon into the carton and then took a bite of ice cream.

"But there's something else, isn't there?" Gabriel said. All Jeremy could do was squeeze the can of soda as he took in the exchange between his brother and Elizabeth.

"Hey, Shaunty," Elizabeth said. "Slide on down, honey, and bring your ice cream, and let's go in the living room and watch some TV."

Mother and daughter moved into the living room, and he heard the TV flick on. He pulled in a breath just as Gabriel leaned on the counter closer to him, his expression amused.

"Well, spill," Gabriel said. "What is it? Girls, money, school, Dad…" He gestured between them. "Is this about your boss and the women you work with, or is it something else?"

"You know my friend Alex?"

Gabriel nodded.

"Well, he has a sister I haven't seen in years, and I kind of ran into her tonight. Actually, I didn't really run into her. It was more like two ships passing in the night."

Gabriel raised a brow, and he could see he didn't get it.

"I spotted her on the way here at the traffic light, and I haven't thought about her in years, but then just seeing her as she drove past and remembering that night and being with her…" He took in Gabriel's amused expression, the way he raised his brows. He knew his brother got it.

"I see," Gabriel said, "and you want to see her, or…?"

He could see his brother was having trouble understanding, which was exactly the same trouble Jeremy was having. He shouldn't care.

"I don't know," he said. "It's just kind of weird, is all. After we hooked up, it was a night of fun, and then we went our separate ways. It was just a one-night stand kind of thing, by the lake, being as she's Alex's sister and it shouldn't have happened in the first place. But there was something about her, and maybe it was just that night— but then one day she was just gone. I remember not seeing her and saying something to Alex, and he just said she had gone to live with their aunt, moved away. He never said anything else." *And I could never ask.*

"So Alex doesn't know you were with his sister?" Gabriel said.

Jeremy pulled his gaze away and looked over his shoulder to see Elizabeth and Shaunty focused on the TV, not him. "Seriously? It's not the kind of thing you tell your best friend, like, 'Hey, Alex, remember that night down at the lake when I snuck off with your sister? Well, guess what? We kind of hooked up.'" He lifted the soda and drained it before setting the can down and taking in the confusion on his brother's face. "He'd kill me if he knew," Jeremy finally said and leaned on the counter, feeling the tightness pull across his shoulders.

"So I don't understand," Gabriel said. "You're going to ask her out, is that it? Or are you going to tell Alex, or…?"

Well, that was a no. Telling his friend was nowhere in the realm of possibility. Alex could never know, but at the same time, Jeremy was toying with the notion of mentioning he'd spotted Tiffy in town, something along the lines of *Hey, didn't know she was back in town—and yeah, can you give me her number so I can call her?* Then what? That certainly wasn't going to work.

"See you're having some trouble, Jeremy, and I don't remember you ever mentioning a girl more than once," Gabriel said. "If you're curious, call her, stop by and see her. Maybe she's just visiting, and remember, too, she could also be married or involved with someone. So then you'd best move on. You ever stop to think that she told her brother about you two already, and maybe he knows?"

That had him sitting up a lot straighter. He hadn't thought of her hooking up with someone else, which, of course, was likely. At the same time, he realized with horror that she may have told Alex. As soon as he thought it, he shook it off, because he wouldn't still be in one piece if Alex knew. "Well, you gave me a lot to think about," he said. "Great advice, thanks, but I should get going. Got plans tonight." He stood up from the stool and took in the way Gabriel was shaking his head.

"Advice? Okay, whatever. Not sure what it was I said, but hey, listen to this: Messing around with your best friend's sister is exactly the kind of thing that will have him being your ex-best friend, and that'll be after he kicks your ass from one side of town to the other. So tread carefully. I can see even in your way of saying nothing that you're going to do what you're going to do, and it doesn't matter what anyone says. Just use your head and not your…" Gabriel gestured rather crudely, and Jeremy just rolled his eyes as he turned away and started into the living room.

"Elizabeth, Shaunty, great to see you," he said as he went to the front door and pulled it open, then stepped out and down the steps.

"Hey, Jeremy, word of advice," Gabriel said from behind him, "since I'm sure you're likely going to do something you shouldn't."

Jeremy stopped on the sidewalk halfway to his truck, parked out front on the street, and looked up to Gabriel standing on the porch. He said nothing and took in the slow amused smile that touched his brother's lips.

"You should just call her."

He just stared at his brother, remembering again how soft Tiffy's lips were, her perfect breasts, and the edge of danger that had come with sneaking off with her.

"Later" was all he said before he continued to his

truck. Then he climbed behind the wheel and picked up his phone, seeing a text from Alex.

Bring snacks!!

CHAPTER
Three

J eremy grabbed two large bags of Doritos, thinking of the keg at Kurt's house—well, Kurt's parents' house, actually. Even though the guy was a dick, the parties were always at his house. He spotted a bag of Miss Vickies malt vinegar chips and grabbed that, as well. He was thinking of grabbing a package of jerky as he made his way over to the deli when he spotted Tiffy Cahill, he was sure, taking a package of cold cuts from one of the deli clerks.

Her hair was longer, pinned back at the sides, and he had to tell himself to keep walking, to breathe and put one foot in front of the other. He cut through the tables of baked goods as she tucked the package into her red grocery basket. He'd ask her out, maybe tonight, and skip the party.

He was so close, and she turned, flicking her eyes up, the odd hazel that was a shade darker than her brother's. She wore a tank top with a gray cardigan and faded blue jeans, and he realized she was looking right at him, and the smile she'd worn seconds earlier had faded. There was no recognition, and she pulled her gaze away as if she hadn't even seen him.

Damn, he couldn't believe it. How could she have forgotten? She was walking away.

"Tiffy," he called even though he knew he shouldn't. He should let her go, let her walk away. He should just pay for his junk food and get the hell out of the store before Alex learned what he did to his sister.

He saw her freeze about ten steps from him. Her back stiffened before she turned, and he could see she couldn't hide her reaction to him.

"Hi," he said. "I thought I saw you at the lights in town."

She turned around fully, holding her basket, but there was no friendly smile, nothing that said she knew him.

She opened her mouth, he thought to say something, but instead she let out a breath as he stepped closer again. *Awkward* was all he could think. She had to know who he was. How could she not? He took in her curves as his gaze swept over the body he remembered, the same full pink lips, her perfect chin. She wasn't looking right at him. It was an awkward glance to the side, down and to the baked goods, before her gaze landed back on him.

"Yes?" was all she said, as if he were a stranger.

Like, what the fuck?

"It's been a long time," he said. The last time he'd seen her, she'd been naked under him on a blanket outside at the lake, a night he swore he'd never forget.

There it was, a tight smile. "Yes, I suppose. Well, I have to get going. I'm…" She gestured over her shoulder and started to step back, her lips firmed. "Take care" was all she said, not *Great to see you! How are you?* or anything of the polite conversation he'd expected. He realized there was not a chance of anything happening between them, which was just as well.

He just stood there, holding those damn Doritos and a bag of Miss Vickies, and watched as Tiffy Cahill hurried away to one of the cashiers. She set the basket on the counter and unloaded her groceries, then looked up and back over to him. What he saw staring back at him for a second confused the hell out of him, because it seemed as if she was angry. Really? She pulled her gaze away and flicked a smile to the cashier before paying.

He felt so many things in that second. He'd never been so confused in all his life. *Women!* was all he could think before his phone dinged again, and he knew it was likely Alex wondering where the snacks were.

He could hear music from the two-story gray house where cars were parked up and down the street. It was an older area of town, ultra conservative, and he wondered how the neighbors handled the craziness that often came from Kurt's.

He pulled past the already packed driveway and took a spot in front of a modest bungalow as the sun slipped lower on the horizon, and then he slipped out of his pickup and grabbed the bag of snacks before the family that lived there could come out and tell him to move it.

"Hey, Jeremy!" he heard a couple of girls call out, standing with a few jocks in front of the house. He lifted his hand in a wave as he walked in through the open door and past the crowd of what appeared to be a hundred, easy, stuffed into the house. The living room was jammed, as were the hallway and the stairwell, as he made his way to the back of the house, where the kitchen was filled and the keg was being manned by Kurt himself.

"Jeremy, you made it," Kurt said.

"Yeah," he said and looked around. It sounded as if Kurt was well on his way. He took a plastic cup filled with the warm draft. "You seen Alex?" he asked, but Kurt was already talking to someone else.

He spotted Boone Hudson just out the back with a couple blondes, and it took him a second to stop himself from walking out there and getting in his face. He still couldn't believe what the jerk had done to his sister Chelsea with that sex tape. He still wanted to cause Boone a lot of misery, even though Chelsea's fiancé, Ric, had made sure the harassment stopped.

"'Bout time you got here," Alex said, ripping the bag of Miss Vickies from Jeremy's hands and tossing it to Kurt before taking both bags of Doritos. "What took you so long?"

Alex was his height and build. His hair, though, was on the longish side and lighter than Jeremy's. His face was the same oval shape as his sister's, with a light spattering of freckles, and his eyes were glassy as he ripped open the bag of Doritos, spilling some on the floor.

"Stopped in to see my brother and at the store for your dinner," Jeremy said. He took in Alex's goofy grin as he shoved a handful of chips in his mouth. Yup, he definitely had no idea what he and Tiffy had done. He lifted the cup and took a swallow of the warm draft, wishing it were cold.

"Listen," Alex said. "I'm going out with Sky tomorrow, movies, dinner, and her cousin is in town, so I kind of need you to step in and be her date. Show up so she's not the third wheel."

Jeremy took in his friend, not wanting to tag along either. Sky was a blond airhead, as far as he was concerned, and being around the two of them was painful at times, considering they spent more time making out than anything else.

He shook his head. "Yeah, no thanks. Not into punishing myself, and I have a policy of never doing blind dates." He didn't need to search that hard for a woman, and he was still smarting from the blow-off from Tiffy.

"Ah, come on," Alex said. "Look, Sky's been making all kinds of excuses and won't go out unless her cousin comes, and those two always end up slipping off together, and I end up going home alone with a night of nothing more than holding hands. You owe me." He shoved another handful of Doritos in his mouth as he was bumped by one of the jocks trying to get over to the keg. Jeremy's beer spilled down his shirtfront.

"Shit..." He wiped his jeans and downed the rest of the draft before he spilled more on himself. "I owe you nothing, and seriously, I'm not interested in entertaining some chick all night who's likely..."

"She's hot," Alex cut in. "Like, smokin'." He gestured to imitate the size of her breasts. At any other time, that would've been all Jeremy needed, so why was he still considering saying no?

"Yeah, better not. Got to work," he added, though he didn't, really, other than to stop in, and then what? He took in the way his friend shook his head and shoved more Doritos in his mouth. He wondered how long ago Alex had started on the beer and whatever else. "Hey, I thought I saw your sister today..." he started. What was he doing? There was something about Alex's mouth now, and he knew he was toying with danger.

Alex tilted his head back and devoured what Jeremy thought must have been crumbs left in the bag of Doritos. Then he crumpled the bag and tossed it over the head of some guy Jeremy had never seen before at the counter. Alex pulled the back of his hand over his mouth to wipe away the crumbs.

"Yeah, she's been home about a week," he said. He swept his hand in the air as if it was nothing. "You seriously can't find time to show up at least for the movie or dinner, an hour? Come on. Sky is seriously not going to leave her at home alone, and she already said her cousin won't tag along as a third wheel. I'll owe you big time." Alex was never going to leave it alone, and Jeremy finally shrugged.

"An hour." He couldn't believe he'd said it. "But no movie."

Alex fisted his hands in the air. "Seriously, you're killing me…"

Jeremy only shook his head, still stuck on Tiffy when he should've been heading over to the keg for another beer. "So where has your sister been? I mean, she up and moved away how long ago? She moving back for good?" Okay, what was wrong with him? He took in something in Alex's expression as he paused and then pulled in a breath. Jeremy wasn't sure what he was thinking as he shrugged.

"Family stuff," he replied. "Listen, I don't want to talk about my sister. She's back, but now I have to give up my games room, because it's not just her, and our cozy bungalow is becoming overcrowded."

So she was attached, married, a boyfriend. Whatever, didn't matter. Taken was taken, and he needed to move on and get her the hell out of his mind. It was only because she wouldn't give him the time of day. That was the only reason he was acting like a sex-starved puppy.

"Well, maybe I can come for more than an hour tomorrow," he said. He'd give it a chance, and maybe this cousin of Sky's would be all he needed to shift his attention from Tiffy and a night he'd never forget.

"Hey, great, what changed your mind?" Alex now wore a big wide goofy smile.

The fact that your sister is taken, and I need to find a way to redirect my interest. "To help you out, and Sky's cousin better be all you say."

"That's great. Hey, listen, if you're crashing tonight, too, you're going to have to take the couch, because Tiffy and my nephew have the futon in my games room."

Then Alex was grabbed from behind by a couple of rowdy friends, and beer was flowing, and Jeremy was still stuck on *nephew*.

CHAPTER
Four

Tiffy missed her bed. Being forced to sleep on a futon, and a hard one, at that, was another reason she was up before anyone else in her parents' house. She blinked at the sliver of light that poked through the blinds, and she took in her dark-haired little boy beside her, fast asleep. She realized some of the discomfort she was feeling was because the bed was wet. Her decision to give in and let him wear his big-boy underwear to bed instead of a pull-up had been exactly the wrong choice.

She rolled off the futon, her bare feet hitting the beige carpet, taking in her brother's big-screen TV and PS4, which now filled the room that had once been her bedroom. Tiffy Jean Cahill had always been strong minded, strong willed, and had a somewhat difficult personality, as her mother put it. She kept so much of what she was feeling and doing to herself. Even her brother, a year older than her, didn't have a clue where her head was at, and that was just fine with Tiffy.

She'd made her own bed, as her dad often said. The

result could be either an epic failure or something else, depending on the circumstances she'd created, which she often chalked up to *What the hell were you thinking?* Her decisions were something she didn't share with anyone.

She pulled at her pajama shorts and the T-shirt she'd slept in before pushing her dark hair over her shoulders as she yawned, taking in the clutter of her open suitcase on the floor and the white garbage bag filled with dirty clothes for her and Brandon. She reached for a pull-up from the package tossed on the open suitcase and knelt on the bed. Without waking her little boy, she peeled off his soaked underwear and slipped on the diaper. He stirred and murmured but didn't wake, and for a second she found herself taking in how he was the image of his father more and more every day.

She reached for the plastic bag and tucked in his underwear, knowing she was running out of clean clothes for Brandon. She would have to wait until everyone was awake before she started the washer, considering it was a twenty-year-old model that clanged and rocked and could be heard everywhere in the house. She let out a breath and pulled open the door, then paused in the hallway of the quiet bungalow, seeing her parents' door closed at the end of the hall. Her brother's across the hall was also closed.

She was first up, and she walked in the bathroom and shut the door. She took her time and then washed her hands, taking in the dark circles under her eyes, the tiny imperfections on her face, and her hair, which needed another wash. First, coffee and some quiet so she could figure out everything about her day and remind herself she'd made the right choice in moving back here. Home was home, and Brandon was at an age where she would need help from her family.

She pulled open the bathroom door and stopped in the open doorway, seeing the futon and a sleeping Brandon in what had been her bedroom until she left almost three years earlier. Her brother, she noted, had wasted no time in taking over, and her parents had let him. She just shook her head again, thinking of the single bed she'd once had, a girl's bed, and here she had returned as a woman, a mother.

Tiffy strode barefoot toward the kitchen, the hardwood creaking with each step. She yawned as she took in the living room, which was open to the kitchen, and froze when she saw the male on the sofa, his chest bare. Good God, was it impressive! He had dark hair and a messy five o'clock shadow, and his arm was tossed over his eyes. He was asleep.

Jeremy Friessen…shit!

She looked right and then left, seeing the kitchen, the door, and the hallway that led back to where her little boy was. She took a step backward and somehow bumped the hall table, and she whirled around, reaching for the vase as it tipped. She righted it and held her breath, mentally kicking herself, trying to be so quiet.

When she turned around, Jeremy was watching her. His eyes were that amazing green, and he had killer abs she didn't remember. Those lips…shit, she wished he'd pull the blanket up and cover all that perfection. Why the hell was he there in her living room, her parents' living room?

"Tiffy" was all he said, and he was looking right at her.

She had to remind herself to breathe. "So you're sleeping on the sofa. Why?" she said, a little too sharply, and she wasn't sure what she saw in the flicker in his eyes. This was a Jeremy she didn't remember, and seeing him yesterday had damn near gutted her. She was still affected, and that just couldn't happen.

"I don't drink and drive," he said. "So you moved away and now you're back, to stay?" he added and sat up, the blanket falling away. She let out a sigh of relief when she saw he'd slept in his jeans. He lifted his arms and stretched his bare feet onto the floor, then stood up and reached for a shirt tossed at the other end of the sofa. She realized she was staring as he pulled on a Cubs T-shirt, and then he was really looking at her. Of course, she hadn't answered. What could she say? Yes, she was back, because it was time, and she figured it was safe.

"Yup…yup…" she said, crossing her arms, feeling naked in front of him. "I'm looking for a place and a job." She hadn't considered that she'd ever run into Jeremy, not like this.

"So…where did you go to? One day you were just gone." He crossed his arms, and she couldn't keep her traitorous eyes from going right to his magnificent chest, to those arms, and she needed to end this now.

"Just away, to family, you know, trying a new place, a new town."

They were still talking when she should've been finding a way to get him out the door.

"Mommy, I want pancakes!" Her son came running behind her, yelling, and grabbed her legs. His smile was precious, and she rested her hand on his short dark hair, which was sticking up on the side. His two-year-old baby teeth flashed.

"No pancakes today. How about a bowl of cereal and some orange juice?" she said, and her son glanced up and over to Jeremy.

"Okay." He jumped, still holding her legs. "Who are you?" He was so quick, and she took in Jeremy, who was looking at her son, staring at him. She didn't know what to make of the expression on his face.

"I'm Jeremy, and you are?" He actually took a step to her son, who still had one hand wrapped around her leg and both feet standing on hers.

"Brandon," he said, and there was that Jeremy smile, the same one that would, at one time, have had her willing and ready to do anything. She had to look away.

"Come on, you. Let's get you some breakfast and me some coffee," she said and lifted Brandon up. He wrapped his legs around her waist, and she patted his pull-up as she walked into the open-concept kitchen and pulled open the cupboard. She reached for a box of cereal and rested it on the counter, seeing that Jeremy had followed her in and was now leaning on the island, watching her with far too much interest. She reached for a bowl in the cupboard and a spoon in the drawer before pulling open the fridge and grabbing the milk. Then she walked over to the small dinette by the sliding glass doors.

"Okay, sit down and let Mommy pour your cereal. Do you want just half full, full, or really full?" she said as she sat her little boy on the chair. He sat on his knees, and Jeremy pulled out a chair across from him at the small round table. She couldn't look at him, and she struggled to hold it together as she poured milk into the bowl. She had to remind herself he'd leave soon…right? Like, what the hell, Alex? She wanted to have a word with her brother about bringing his stray friends home.

"So, Brandon, how old are you?" she heard Jeremy say, and she jabbed the spoon in the cereal and slammed the drawer harder than was necessary.

"Okay, Brandon, here's your breakfast. Eat up, and I'll get you some orange juice," she said and put the bowl in front of her son, seeing the way Jeremy's eyes went from her son to her where she stood with her hand on the back of Brandon's chair.

He held up two fingers as he shoveled a mouthful of cereal in, the milk spilling out.

"You're two? Wow, you're almost grown up," Jeremy teased, and there was something about the way he did that to her son that brought a feeling of anger bubbling inside her. She squeezed the back of the chair and took in the way Jeremy's green eyes flicked up to her. His hooded gaze hid everything.

She had to fight the urge to ball her fist, because she wanted nothing more than to slug him and all that arrogance. She pushed away and walked back over to the fridge, then yanked it open and grabbed the carton of orange juice, feeling how light it was. She gave it a shake, and there was only a dribble in there.

"Alex…" she said under her breath. She gave the door of the fridge a shove closed. "How about some milk instead, Brandon? It looks like your uncle drank all the juice and put an empty carton back in the fridge."

"I hear my name…" Her brother strode into the kitchen, bare-chested and stinking of beer, and he went over to Brandon and tousled his hair, then took his spoonful of cereal and shoved it in his own mouth.

"Hey, that's mine!" Brandon said and laughed, and Alex stood up and wiped his mouth with the back of his hand.

She held up the carton as if it said everything, and Alex just shrugged as he walked over to the coffee pot and started making coffee. "I thought for sure you'd have made coffee already. What have you two been doing out here?"

She had to grit her teeth, because the last thing she wanted to do was talk about Jeremy with her brother. She said nothing as she pressed her palms on the island and looked over to him, seeing that he was watching her.

She realized her brother was looking right at her and

then over to Jeremy as he pressed the button and started the coffee brewing. "No one answering? Hey, Jeremy, coffee. How about breakfast, eggs, a pound of bacon? Tonight, you can swing on by here at fivish and follow me over to Sky's and meet her cousin there. She can ride with you, and hopefully you can convince her to…"

Tiffy took in the rude gesture her brother made, and she made herself pull in a deep breath. "Alex, seriously? Brandon is sitting right there," she said.

Her brother shrugged and made a face as he grabbed a spatula and rested a frying pan on the stove.

"You know what, you two? I've got to go," Jeremy said. "I'll skip the breakfast, but thanks for the use of your sofa." He leaned in closer to Brandon and rustled his hair. "Pleasure, Brandon, until we meet again."

Her son laughed, and she fisted her hands and did her best to hold it together as Jeremy stood up and walked into the living room, grabbed his keys and wallet, and stuffed them in his pocket before striding over to the front door and shoving his feet into sneakers.

"Later," he said and pulled open the door, then stepped out.

She shut her eyes for a second and let out a breath that she hadn't realized she'd been holding. Then she flicked her eyes open and turned, taking in her brother, who was watching her intently and then staring at the door Jeremy had just walked through.

"What was that?" Alex jabbed the metal spatula right at her, and she had to fight the urge to flinch.

"What are you talking about?" she said, walking over to her son, who was done his cereal and had lifted his bowl to drink the milk, which was running down the side of his mouth. "Brandon, no…" she said as she pulled the bowl away and reached for a cloth napkin folded in the middle of the table. She wiped his face and then the milk on the table and chair before she helped him down. "Come on, let's get you cleaned up," she said as Brandon ran into the living room and went to pull out the box of toys that had once belonged to her brother, which her mom had pulled out of the attic. He pulled out the truck and cars.

"Tiffy, seriously, what the hell was that about?" Alex took a step toward her, and the way he was watching her, she could see he was thinking. Then he shifted his gaze to Brandon and put down the spatula on the island before pulling his hand across his face. He dragged his finger from her to the door and back.

"You and Jeremy?" was all he said.

She pulled her tongue over her teeth, keeping her mouth closed, and his gaze landed on Brandon again.

"Tiffy, uh…" he said, and she could see the minute he got it. "You and my best friend…and Brandon?" She could see the flash of fury and the way the anger seemed to roll off him in waves. He rolled his shoulders. "I'll kill him," he said, so matter of fact, as he walked around the island and down the hall to his bedroom. She glanced once to Brandon and then started after her brother, who was pulling on a T-shirt and socks.

"Alex, what are you doing?" She stepped into his room, which smelled just as bad as he did.

He turned on her, and she didn't miss the anger on his face. "What am I doing? You're serious? I don't know why I didn't figure it out and put it together before. But now, having the two of them together in the same room, he looks just like Jeremy. I should have figured it out as soon as I saw Brandon. It's the eyes. Christ, he knocks you up and bails and then gets to fuck off while you're off across the country at Aunt Rita's, having a kid, and I never figured it out. I'll tell you what I'm doing."

He reached for his keys and his wallet, which were buried under a pile of clothes on a desk in the corner. "I'm doing what I should have done three years ago, because guys don't mess around with their best friend's sister, not ever. I'll kill him." His finger was in front of her face, and then he walked around her, and she could feel the anger oozing from him. Add in the liquor he reeked of still, and she knew this was exactly what couldn't happen.

"Alex, wait, stop right now. You can't do this…" She ran after him to the front door, seeing her son, Jeremy's son, pulling out all the toys. But her brother was already out the door and into his faded blue Subaru, which was parked at an odd angle.

He backed out of the driveway with a squeal and then pulled away.

"Is that your brother driving like a crazed person, waking up half the neighborhood again?" Her mom asked from behind her, wearing a short blue and black kimono robe over her wide frame. Her blond hair hung in waves over her shoulders, and she went over to Brandon, touching his head and then leaning down and kissing him when he smiled up at her. "Good morning, my sweet boy," she said.

Tiffy closed the door, pulling in her lower lip between her teeth when her mom glanced her way. She hadn't answered. "Yeah, he's, uh… You know Alex," she said.

Her mom rolled her eyes as she strode into the kitchen, and her dad appeared too in an identical robe that stopped mid-thigh, kissing her mom. Then they were both in the kitchen, laughing, doing what her parents always did. To them, nothing was ever a big deal, and they had always let her and Alex pretty much do whatever they wanted.

That was also why she was, she figured, in the predicament she was in now. But they were right about one thing: This was her life, her choices, and she needed to figure out what the hell to do—because the last thing she wanted was for Jeremy Friessen to ever find out that Brandon was his son.

CHAPTER

Five

Something wasn't adding up. Seeing Tiffy and her two-year-old son, he had realized it was just the two of them, no one else, no boyfriend or guy there with her. Was she newly divorced, separated, or had she just hooked up with the wrong guy and was now, from what he could tell, a single mom with a kid at eighteen? What a way to start out her young adult life. It must have been a mess for her. Why was he still thinking about her and giving her the time of day?

He parked his truck beside his dad's pickup and Gabriel's older model, which was still newer than his own pickup. He gave his door a shove as he walked toward the house, hearing voices from the barn and the house. As the screen door opened, out stepped his sister.

"You didn't come home last night, Jeremy," Sarah said. "Dad was just asking about you, and Mom, too. We were all wondering where you were, especially when Mom said your bed wasn't slept in. She was going to call you, but Dad said to leave it alone and you'd show up." She strode out of the house, her very light blond hair pulled back in a high ponytail, wearing blue jeans and a faded yellow T-shirt. She was getting into his business just like she did everyone's.

He made a face as he glanced to the barn and ran his hand over his hair, which was a mess and likely sticking up everywhere. He needed a shower, getting a whiff of how bad he smelled, and to brush his teeth and have a coffee. "Crashed at Alex's. Where is everyone?" he asked, thinking of the date he'd committed himself to later.

It was a favor Alex was going to owe him for big time, considering Jeremy still wasn't convinced it would be anything other than time he'd never get back. There was just something about the idea of a blind date that didn't interest him in the least. He was the last guy who'd ever need anyone to fix him up. He liked it that way.

"Gabriel and Dad and Zach were rounding up some of the calves early this morning, and Elizabeth and Shaunty are here. Elizabeth brought a bunch of crabapples, so we're making jelly right now. Mom's been canning since yesterday, and…"

He turned his head to the barn even though his sister was still talking, filling him in on everything she seemed to think he was missing. His dad and Gabriel were leading the horses out to one of the corrals to graze, and he'd stopped listening to Sarah, who could, at times, go on about everything, giving a blow by blow, with details that he didn't want to hear.

Then he heard a car and turned to see the dust in the distance and what looked like a small blue Subaru. Alex. Seriously? Like, he'd just left his place. Had he forgotten something? Yup, the closer he got, he could see it was his friend, who always drove on the fast side. It was just something about Alex, nothing calm and reasonable. He was about getting places fast, not wasting time, go big or go home. But the way he was coming in was crazed, out of control, and unusually over the top, even for Alex.

He took the curve in the dirt road so fast his back end skidded around. The rev of his engine was loud, and Jeremy could hear the door to the house behind him, but he didn't glance back. Alex's hands were white on the wheel, and he was staring right at him, coming right for him, not slowing at all. Like, what the fuck? This crazy-ass shit was not the thing to pull here, not around his dad, his family.

He just stood there and could hear his mom yell behind him, he thought. Then his sister and someone else shouted, and all he could think was that his friend wasn't slowing down, and he was so close, coming closer still, in this bizarre, twisted, fucked-up scenario that he couldn't wrap his head around. Time froze, and someone was yelling in the distance, long and loud, before he was hit from the side, arms around him, and he was tackled hard. It knocked the wind out of him, and he was on the ground with an *oomph*.

He gasped, pulling the dust that whirled around them deep into his lungs. It was in that second that he realized the car had now stopped so close that he could reach out and touch the front end of the dingy chrome, which he thought was steaming. It was another second before he realized it was his dad who had knocked him out of the way. He was on the ground beside him, and Jeremy sat up, coughing, seeing the faded blue of the Subaru and then Alex stalking around the car toward him, his face contorted with rage. He was pumped and furious.

What the hell had he missed? His best friend's hands were fisted.

"You son of a bitch!" Alex yelled. "I swear to God, you are so dead…" Then he ran, blasting a warrior yell at

Jeremy and landing a punch to his face, his nose. Then he was on top of him, yelling, as he felt the pounding of a fist, one, two. Then Alex was yanked off him.

Jeremy tasted blood and saw Gabriel and his dad pulling a twisting, out of control, furious Alex off him. He wasn't the happy-go-lucky friend he'd left less than an hour ago, on whose sofa he'd slept all night. Then he felt hands on his shoulders and beside him, his mom and Elizabeth, who helped him up.

"What is this about?" his dad yelled. "Settle down, Alex! What is wrong with you, coming in here like you did, driving like a maniac? You could have killed someone! You were headed right for Jeremy, and you'd have hit him if I hadn't knocked him out of the way. You're angry about something? I don't care what this is! Knock it off!"

He could see Alex struggling, and Gabriel and his dad had to fight to hold him back. "Let me at him! You are so dead, Jeremy! You motherfucker, you touched my sister? You son of a bitch, you knocked her up and then fucked off on her? You think you get a pass and can screw my sister and treat her like some two-dollar whore and then run, and you think I'm going to call you a friend and let you get away with that shit?"

Everyone was staring at him, and he couldn't get past what his friend was saying. He'd never seen the hate, the violence, on anyone's face before—not for him. Alex knew about Tiffy, and he was insinuating…what, that he was somehow the father? No.

"Hey, wait! Okay, I admit I slept with her, but you're wrong about the kid. I would never do what you're saying! You're saying I got her pregnant, yet this is the first I'm hearing of this. You're wrong. Did your sister tell you…?"

His dad was looking from him to Alex and not saying a word. Gabriel appeared furious, shocked, maybe, still holding a fighting Alex, who was trying to break out of their grasp.

"You son of a bitch, I'll kill you! You calling my sister a liar? Don't you fucking dare say one word or try and worm your way out of what you did. In fact, she said nothing. I figured it out. I bet you were laughing behind my back, you fucking prick, knowing all this time what you did to my sister and thinking you got away with it! The only thing you've done is gotten on my bad side and made an enemy for life. How the fuck did I not figure this out before?" Alex was yelling, and Jeremy didn't have to look over to the three shocked, likely traumatized faces of Sarah, Zach, and Shaunty, who shouldn't have been hearing any of this. Yet they were glued to the scene as if his life were one of those explosive action movies and they couldn't pull their eyes away from the screen.

"The way you two were with each other this morning, I knew something was up, and three years ago when she left, moved away, pregnant, thinking it was better to have the baby somewhere else where no one knew her, saying she just wanted a new start and didn't want her friends to see her pregnant when they were all talking prom dresses and evening gowns, lipstick and mascara, and she's looking at maternity wear and childbirth… Mom and Dad let her go even though they would have loved nothing more than to have her at home. It was just a baby, they said, no big deal, but she moved in with my aunt, saying she wanted the anonymity. Now I know, it was because of you that she left. Because you fucked her over!" Alex was breathing heavy.

Jeremy felt a cloth touch his lip, feeling the sting, and pulled back. His mom was there, holding a rag. Her mouth was set firmly, and the way she was watching him was filled with outrage, disappointment, and likely the same shock he was feeling. He took the cloth from her, and she didn't pull her gaze from him.

"You're wrong, Alex. He's not my kid," Jeremy said. He couldn't be.

His dad was looking at him with an expression he'd never seen before, his eyes narrowed. Sarah, Zach, and Shaunty were on the porch, so quiet, hanging over the railing, shocked. Elizabeth was on the other side of him, staring over to Gabriel, who said something to Alex. Right now, he wanted to be anywhere but there. He spit blood on the ground after pulling the cloth away from his bleeding lip.

"Settle down right now!" Andy said. "Do I need to call the sheriff, or are you going to behave yourself?" He was putting everything into holding Alex back, keeping Alex from launching at him again and using his fists on him. He'd never seen this side of his friend, this kind of anger, hate. It was so wrong, but then, so was the fact that Alex believed Tiffy's little boy was his. What was his name again? He couldn't remember. Alex had to be wrong.

"Fine, just let go of me," Alex said. His face was red with rage, but Andy and Gabriel let him go, though they were still right beside him, ready to grab him if he moved any closer to Jeremy. Alex squeezed his fists at his sides and shuffled his stance as if doing his best to pull it the fuck together. Then he let out a breath before holding up his hands as if to show them he'd heard them and would refrain from jamming his fists in Jeremy's face again.

"And you?" Andy snapped, leveling his hardened gaze on Jeremy. Those icy blue eyes could cut right through bullshit. "What is this about a kid, you getting some girl pregnant?" His dad was staring straight at him and then back to Alex.

"Look, I don't know anything about what Alex is

accusing me of, or me getting Tiffy pregnant," he said. "Yes, I had sex with Tiffy...how long ago? And yeah, you're right, I'm a total dog for that, but there's no way I would ever do what you're saying, knock up a girl and then walk! Tiffy never said one word to me. It was a night of fun, we both wanted it, and it meant nothing. The only thing I knew is one day she up and moved away. She left town until I saw her yesterday, and I saw her and the kid today. You're wrong. He's not mine. Did she tell you he was?"

Even Gabriel was giving him a look like he needed to mind what he was saying or he'd take up where Alex had left off. He pressed his hands to his head, bumping a sore spot at his brow, feeling the warm stickiness of blood, reliving that night by the lake and the sex they'd had. Yes, he was a total fuck-up, but he'd used a condom. So yeah, his friend was wrong. There'd been someone else, because there was no way that kid was his.

Alex firmed his lips and shook his head hard. "She didn't have to. I figured it out and should have figured it out when I first saw him. He looks just like you, Jeremy, you fucking lowlife bastard. I put it together. She didn't deny it, and Tiffy doesn't lie. So tell me what you're planning to do about this, you fucker." His friend jabbed his finger his way, and his dad was looking over to his mom, who was still beside him. He didn't have to look down to see how upset she was. The emotion from everyone was over the top.

"Hey, first, I'm done with the threats," Andy stated, cutting in before anyone could say anything, which was great because he couldn't think of one reasonable thing to say. He was still reeling from the shock. "If this is true, it'll be handled, and if this is my grandson..." His dad was shaking his head and then leveled his *You've totally fucked up big time, Jeremy* gaze on him, then jabbed his finger toward him with a force he'd not seen before.

"You go talk to her and find out if this is true," Andy said. "If..." He glanced to Alex, who didn't pull his gaze from Jeremy, one that was still filled with the urge to kick his ass into the next county. It said loud and clear that they were no longer friends. "If any of this is true, the boy will be looked after, and so will Tiffy," Andy said to Jeremy as if he needed to be reminded of how he was supposed to handle things.

"Brandon," Alex said. "My nephew's name is Brandon, and he's two, born June 6. You want to do the math? Because that was all I thought of, driving out here. You know what really gets me is when we found out Tiffy was pregnant, she sat us down in the living room and said it was no one of any importance, over and done, and he would never be part of her life. She was so matter of fact."

Boy, did that sting, and it made absolutely no sense to him.

"Jeremy, you need to go and talk to Tiffy," his mom said. "Get cleaned up, showered, because you stink. Then you go over and talk to her." She had her arms crossed, and her eyes were vivid green.

He felt his stomach tighten, because it was then he realized that Brandon had the exact same eyes as his mom, as him.

Holy fuck! was all he could think. He didn't nod, couldn't get his mouth to form a word past the lump jammed in his throat. In that second, what flashed in his mind was the image of the kid, Brandon, the little boy, the smile, the face from that morning.

He already knew how this was going to go down. Brandon was, in fact, his.

CHAPTER
Six

Over her pajamas, Tiffy was wearing the ugliest sweater Jeremy had ever seen, which he thought had red wine spilled on it, from the color and the odor. Her face was giving nothing away. At the same time, he was aware that her father was standing in the background with the oddest expression on his face, but then, Wayne Cahill had never been a man of many words.

Wayne was pleasant, easygoing, and always had a smile and kind word when he talked to anyone. He was also a man with an amazing sense of humor, always laughing, and he leaned toward the dark sarcastic side, choosing to take life not quite so seriously. It was clear from his expression that he had no idea about any of the shit that had just hit the fan, namely, Jeremy being the father of Brandon. Now he wondered what Tiffy had said.

Right now, she was saying nothing. In fact, she crossed her arms, holding them tight over her chest. Her eyes were a shade of blue that really packed a punch, and she was staring at him now with none of the loving feeling she'd given him that night three years earlier.

"You haven't answered me about Brandon," he said. "Alex said he's mine, but you never told me, you never said a word. You just left town." He wanted to lean in closer but wondered how her dad would react. He could still hear what his dad had said the entire drive over in between the lecture about not pissing where you sleep, and what were you thinking, and do we need to sit you down again and have the safe sex talk. Andy had said that when he spoke with Tiffy, he needed to make sure he listened and didn't walk out the door until he had a plan of action figured out, discussed, and agreed upon. Then there was his mother, who still hadn't said two words to him.

"Tiffy, what is this about?" Wayne said.

Tiffy flicked her gaze over to her dad. It wasn't the kind of look he would have expected, as she shrugged as if none of this was a big deal. "Alex was over at Jeremy's house and is responsible for Jeremy's bashed-in face, all because he figured out Brandon is Jeremy's son. Yes, Jeremy is the father of Brandon. It was a youthful misguided choice on my part, but then, Brandon isn't a mistake, just so we're clear. Jeremy is now here because…" She turned her head back to him and gestured as if he wasn't explaining himself properly. The way she spoke and the way she watched him, nothing in her expression said she was about to have anything to do with him. "Why are you here, Jeremy? Even I knew that night was a one-nighter, no strings, and we went our separate ways. Even if I didn't fully understand it at the time, it became crystal clear not long after. You're a player, and that doesn't fit into my life. Nor is it something I want anywhere around my son," she added.

The way she sounded so calm, he couldn't get his head

around the fact that she'd alluded to something having given her the idea that he was the lowest kind of dog, which he wasn't. "What do you mean, figured out?" he said.

She was too smart, and she was now staring over at her father as if they were discussing something that was of little to no importance. "So yes, Dad, it seems Jeremy is here because Alex is angry his best friend had sex with me, and…" She furrowed her brows as if she was confused, staring back at him, not answering him at all. She'd tossed her own question right back to him.

"Tiffy, this isn't a game," he said. "Why would you think I wouldn't want to know about Brandon? You should have told me about him the minute you found out you were pregnant. I had a right to know. Good God, you were like…"

"Fifteen and a bit. You were sixteen and like a god to me. Look at us now. Guess I woke up," she said, and her words felt as if she'd balled up her fist and rammed it in his gut. It was a sucker punch, too, because she seemed to know exactly what buttons to push. It was as if she was trying to deliberately emasculate him.

"Wayne," Andy said, "we should likely sit down and discuss some things about Tiffy and Brandon."

Tiffy flicked her gaze past him to his dad, stepping to the side around Jeremy and giving all her attention to him. There had been an edge to Andy's voice, and Jeremy knew his dad had to be chomping at the bit to bring this to some sort of reasonable close, treating her like a woman who couldn't decide anything.

"Excuse me, but there's no sitting down and discussing me and Brandon as if I have no idea what's good for my son," Tiffy said. "I can assure you I very much understand everything about us, our life, my situation, and no one, including you and your son, has any say or gets to decide in any way how we're to think, feel, or act. Seriously, did you think you could just talk to my dad as if I'm not even here? Let me be clear: I and I alone get to decide every-thing about my son, not any of you." She dragged her finger in the air past all of them, taking each one of them in with her astute kick-ass gaze.

Jeremy was stunned. No one had ever talked to his dad like that, like, ever.

"Tiffy, hey, this is my grandson we're talking about," Andy said. He sounded so calm, but Jeremy knew well that his voice held an edge of warning.

"Well, hang on a second, here." Wayne lifted his hands in the air as if everyone just needed to dial it back a bit. "Tiffy, Jeremy is Brandon's father?"

Jeremy blinked, because he thought they had already established this fact.

"Yes, Dad," Tiffy said so calmly.

Wayne turned to him and frowned, taking in Jeremy's face, before turning his gaze back to Tiffy. "I guess there is some resemblance, maybe."

Was he kidding? It was the eyes. They were unmis-takable.

"Okay, this is ridiculous," Jeremy said. "You two are talking as if this is no big deal, when it is very much a big deal. You had my kid and said nothing to me. I had a right to know." He tapped his chest with his hand, leaning in, but Tiffy seemed unaffected as she glanced away, though he could see how tightly she was gripping her sweater under her arms.

"I disagree with you, Jeremy. You seem to think you have rights here, or a right to know, for that matter. Before I figured out I was pregnant, you had already moved on to another girl, another conquest. I think it was my brother who bragged about you conquering the Hardy twins, both of them at the same time! This was less than a week after you and I had our sexcapade down by the lake."

He had to blink and could feel his heartbeat kick up, remembering well that night with the twins. He'd thought of it fondly until now. He heard his dad drag his hand over his face with a scrape of whiskers. He somehow didn't think a pat on the shoulder was coming his way.

"Then there was Linda, and Josie, and…shall I go on?" Tiffy said. "You really think that sixteen-year-old Jeremy, who was walking sex, had any interest in hearing that, oops, I was pregnant?"

He was speechless. She'd twisted everything and was making him sound like a piece of work. Even his dad was quiet, and he couldn't pull his gaze from Tiffy. He'd always known she was smart, but she was turning this into a mockery, implying he was abnormally reckless. And he wasn't, he was trying to tell himself.

Tiffy, who was maybe five-foot four, slim, and barefoot, didn't seem as if she had any intention of giving in, being reasonable, or sitting down with him anytime soon to discuss this like two adults.

"God fucking damn it, Tiffy," he snapped, not knowing what else to say. "I want to see my son." He was breathing heavy, and he could feel everyone staring at him as if he'd lost his mind.

CHAPTER
Seven

J eremy ran a towel over his hair and wiped the steam from the bathroom mirror, having taken a really long shower to clear his head. He felt as if an earthquake had torn the ground from beneath his feet. Seriously, a kid! He was also still shaken that Alex had come barreling down the driveway with murder in his eyes.

He took in his face. The skin around his eye was beginning to color, and his jaw and lip were swollen. He spit blood into the sink and continued to dry himself off.

Alex was where? Still in the living room with Gabriel and his dad. Andy had taken the keys to his Subaru, which was likely still parked oddly too close to the house. He still couldn't believe Alex had tried to run him down. If his dad hadn't tackled him and yanked him out of the way, he was positive he'd be lying in the ER now, if not the morgue. He understood clearly what had driven Alex to want to beat him to death with his bare hands, though. Truth be told, if the shoe were on the other foot and a friend had done to his sister what he'd done to Tiffy, he'd need someone to pull him off the deadbeat, too.

There was a tap on the bathroom door.

"You done in there yet?" It was his dad, and he didn't sound impressed.

Jeremy wrapped the beige towel around his waist and pulled open the door, taking in the way his dad stood in the doorway. His hand was resting on the top of the doorframe before he stepped back, allowing Jeremy room to step by. His gaze said everything about how badly Jeremy had fucked up.

"You really screwed the pooch on this one, Jeremy. Like, what the fuck were you doing? Do you have any idea how old she is—or *was* at the time?" Andy was speaking as if he were a greenhorn who'd left the gate open and let the cattle escape.

Jeremy could feel his dad behind him as he walked into his room, the room he'd grown up in, taking in the queen bed and the dark wood furnishings. He didn't want to answer, but his dad wasn't the kind of man who would let him stay silent. He dumped his clothes in his hamper, and Andy closed the door to the bedroom and pressed his hand against it. Jeremy noticed the blood spatter on his dad's T-shirt and faded blue jeans and realized there was a scrape from his elbow and down, likely from the fall when he'd knocked Jeremy out of the way.

"Where's Alex?" He pulled open his chest of drawers and reached for a clean pair of blue jeans, then tossed them on the bed with a clean pair of socks and underwear before pulling out a red and white T-shirt. He just held it, wondering if his dad would take the hint and leave.

"Parked his ass in the living room. Gabriel is there, and so is your mom, talking to him. He's got a right to be upset…"

"Really, Dad, you think I don't know that?" He cut his dad off, noting that he sounded like an asshole. Apparently his dad did, too, as his icy blue eyes were filled with a warning Jeremy should've been smart enough to heed.

"He has a right to a point, Jeremy, is what I was going to say if you'd let me finish. But coming in the way he did, I'm still tempted to call the sheriff and get him on out here, because the problem with that hotheaded young buck is that he's ready to kill you, and if I hadn't yanked you out of the way, he'd have run you down. Then him jumping you the way he did, if we hadn't pulled him off you, he'd have beat you to death. Shall I go on?"

No, he didn't need to continue. Jeremy got it, all of it and then some, and he had to fight the urge to growl. "Do you mind? I need to get dressed," he said, but his dad didn't even blink and made no motion to move from where he was.

"You can wait. Sit down." His dad gestured to the bed. "I have some things to say to you, and you're going to listen." He noted the way his father pointed to the bed. He was going to be heard, but there was something about being told what to do that wasn't sitting right with Jeremy. Stubbornness had taken over his ability to see reason, so he crossed his arms over his bare chest and gave his dad all his attention. Maybe the odd smile that touched his dad's lips had something to do with the fact that he was aware Jeremy was still standing.

"That boy out there, your good friend Alex, who, I might point out, you've been friends with for what seems like forever…you can kiss that friendship goodbye for good. I think you know this without me having to point it out. You made a move on his sister, his younger sister, and to make it worse, you did the one thing you don't ever do with your friends' sisters: hooking up for a night. What were you thinking? Or evidently, you weren't." His dad crossed his arms, leaning now against the door and crossing one of his dusty cowboy boots over the other.

"I didn't plan it. She was just there," Jeremy said. She'd been by the lake with everyone, and her killer smile had made him say the one thing he shouldn't have, *You want to go for a walk?* She'd slipped her hand in his, and they'd snuck off away from the crowd to a spot by the lake where there was no one. He'd never forget the moment her lips first touched his.

Jeremy ran his hand across his jaw and realized his mistake when he felt a sharp shooting pain. He swore under his breath.

His dad groaned and shoved his hand through his hair, which was a mix of dark and gray. Jeremy could see the frustration in his expression.

"She was just there," Andy said. "Are you kidding me? I seriously hope you become a lot more polished than that before we go back out there. Word of advice, don't repeat that to anyone, Alex, his sister, your mom…" His dad let the words linger, and he remembered with a sick feeling in the pit of his stomach the way his mom had looked at him.

"Look, I didn't mean it like that," Jeremy said. "I didn't know I had a kid. She never said one word to me—and is it mine?" Again, likely not the smartest thing to say. He just couldn't help shoving his foot in his mouth again and again, since his head was telling him one thing, but his heart was telling him he knew the boy was his.

"Well, guess you're going to find out, because you're going to talk to the girl—"

"Tiffy," he interrupted.

His dad's icy blue eyes flashed, and he nodded. "Tiffy. You're going to go talk to her and find out about the boy. If he's yours, you will make it right. If this is my grandson—

and I'm saying 'if' because Alex is one hundred percent convinced you're the father, but would this girl lie?"

He just took in his dad. Even though it would be easier to say that maybe she would, he couldn't. He shook his head and ran his hand over his wet hair. "No, Tiffy just doesn't do that. In fact, I saw her yesterday and she did everything to get away from me. If I'm the father, why didn't she tell me?" He shrugged.

His dad seemed to dial it back a bit. Jeremy could see he was thinking. "Well, maybe that's where you should start, and just because of how volatile this is and the fact that I'm not too interested in seeing you on a slab in the morgue, I'm coming along."

"What? No!" he said. He couldn't remember his dad ever treating him as if he was a kid. He wasn't. He was nineteen, had a job, and was even in charge because his boss was confident in his leadership ability. In fact, he still needed to make time today for work.

"Not negotiable, Jeremy. You dug yourself into a situation that has angered your best friend to the point he still wants to kill you, and then there's the girl's father. What is he likely to do to you?"

Okay, he hadn't thought about that. He just stared at his dad, who moved away from the door and gestured to the bed with his chin.

"Get dressed," Andy said. "Get your head together and watch your mouth. And just so we're clear and you know with one hundred percent certainty, you're getting a paternity test so there's no question at all." His dad then yanked open the door, taking him in once more. "And as far as Alex goes, the only words that should come out of your mouth are 'I'm sorry,' and you better mean it."

CHAPTER
Eight

"I don't want to wear a diaper! I'm a big boy."

Brandon was arguing with her as she tried to get him into a pull-up diaper. All his underwear was in the washer, and there he was, yanking on a dirty pair of blue pajama bottoms and going commando. She still needed to get him down for a nap, even though he also argued he didn't need one. She could hear the phone ringing from the other room, and she thought her mom answered.

"Brandon, you just need to wear this until the washer finishes and I get your clothes into the dryer. Then you can take it off. You wet the bed again last night, so I have to wash everything…"

There was a tap on the open bedroom door, which had her looking up from where she squatted in front of her stubborn two-year-old little boy, who argued about everything. It was her mom, dressed in capris and a blue and white striped shirt, her blond hair hanging in thick waves.

"Your brother's on the phone for you, so why don't I trade you and take my grandson?" Her mom held out the phone and stepped into the bedroom, where she lifted Brandon and kissed him everywhere until he giggled.

"Maybe you can convince him to put on the diaper," Tiffy said. Brandon now had a big ear-to-ear grin for his granny.

"Nonsense! He's just fine the way he is, right?" her mom said.

Brandon answered, "Yeah!" His tongue was out, and the sparkle of light in his innocent, precocious green eyes screamed that he wasn't going down without a fight.

"Mom, seriously, he's got nothing on under those dirty PJ bottoms," Tiffy said, still holding the phone, but her mom just rolled her eyes at her.

"Oh, you worry too much about what he's wearing. I used to let you and your brother run around without any clothes on all the time. It's good for you…"

Now she wanted to roll her eyes. Flo Cahill had always been of the mind to live and let live, never much following what society said.

Her mom put down Brandon, who ran to where the toys were scattered everywhere, taking over the living room so it now resembled a daycare. Flo laughed as she followed him but then stopped in the doorway, her hand resting on the doorframe as she leaned back in. "And find out from your brother if he's planning on being home for dinner. I'll throw a ham in. If not, your dad will cook up some chicken."

Tiffy just stared at her mom, wondering what the difference was between ham or chicken.

Her mom gestured to the phone as if everything she'd said made a world of sense. "Well, go on, talk to your brother, and then you should go run a bath, add some bubbles, and just chill out for a bit. Brandon's fine." She let her gaze run over Tiffy, who was still in her pajama shorts and T-shirt, but at least she'd found a brush and had run it through her hair.

She pressed the phone to her ear. "What's up?" she said.

"First, don't yell."

The minute he said it, she felt her stomach knot up, and she was sure her blood pressure spiked. "What did you do, and where are you?" she said. She could hear him breathing on the other end, and she thought she could hear voices in the background.

"I'm out at Jeremy's, and I may have done something I shouldn't have."

She could feel her throat thicken and her eyes bug out. Alex had always been known for doing something he shouldn't. "Alex, so help me, if you told Jeremy about…"

"I may have tried to hurt Jeremy, and I kind of lost it, so much so that I'm stuck out at the ranch. Jeremy's dad took my keys, and the sheriff is now here babysitting me along with Jeremy's brother Gabriel. I asked to use the phone, so I'm calling you to warn you."

The sheriff? What the fuck, Alex? She couldn't get the words out of her mouth as she squeezed the phone. She remembered all too well Alex's face when he'd run out of the house, threatening to kill Jeremy. She'd just hoped he would realize he was over-reacting and would come to his much-needed senses, stop, and turn around and come on home, where he could stay the hell out of her business. Guess not! "Ah…" was all she could get out, because this was beginning to feel like an impending train wreck.

"Are you still there?" he said.

She realized now what she was picking up in his voice: worry for her. "Yeah, I'm just wondering why you felt the need to shove your nose in my business. So what are you warning me about? I'm hoping you kept the bit about

Brandon being Jeremy's to yourself." She bit the words out, then pulled the phone away and stared at the receiver for a second before pressing it back to her ear.

"Afraid not. He should know, Tiffy. Like, what the fuck were you thinking, not saying anything? I mean, I still want to kill him for touching you…"

She could hear a man in the background, she thought, saying something to her brother. "Alex, what are you doing? What did he say?" she snapped.

"The sheriff was just warning me about issuing threats, saying if something happens to Jeremy, I've just signed my one-way ticket to life behind bars," he said as if it were no big deal.

She pulled the phone away and leaned her head back, wanting to scream at the ceiling but knowing her son was just outside the bedroom and would hear her. She pressed the phone back to her ear, as she could hear her brother talking again.

"And you," he said. "What were you thinking, sleeping with my friend?"

There it was, why she'd planned for no one to ever know.

"Regardless," he said, "Jeremy and his dad are on their way over to the house right now to see you and Brandon, to have a sit-down with you and find out everything."

"Jeremy and his dad?" she snapped, pressing her hand to her wrinkled T-shirt and stepping out of the bedroom to see her mom on all fours in the living room with Brandon, laughing and playing. Her dad was sitting on a bar stool at the kitchen island, drinking coffee and reading a paper, his dark-rimmed glasses perched at the end of his nose. He glanced up as she hurried past to the laundry room behind the kitchen, where the washer was just finishing up.

"Yup, both," Alex said. "The cat's out of the bag, Tiffy,

so you're going to need to deal with him. Truth time. Talk to him, but by no means does he get a pass——"

"Tiffy, Jeremy and his dad are here to see you!" her mom called out, and she just stood where she was in the laundry room, feeling the floor beneath her soften and wanting nothing more than to stay right where she was and hide, say nothing at all, and hope everyone would just forget she was there.

"Well, they're here," she hissed. "You know what, Alex? Thank you very much for sticking your nose in my business and telling Jeremy about Brandon when you had no right. I may have screwed him, but I had my reasons for not saying anything."

He pulled in a breath, ready to argue with her.

"I've got to go," she said and pressed the end button before her brother could say one more word about how he'd just yanked the rug right out from under her and she was supposed to be just fine with it.

Then she took in what she was wearing: a T-shirt, no bra, and just her PJ shorts. She was decent enough for the house, but not for company, even though she knew her mom would tell her to stop worrying about it. To her, it mattered, so she dumped the phone on top of the washer as she looked around the laundry room and saw a black and white polka-dot cardigan that belonged to her mom in the laundry hamper. Shaking it out, she spotted what looked like red wine spilled over it and took a sniff. Yup. But she saw nothing else, so she gave it a shake as if that would help before pulling it on and stepping into the kitchen.

She could hear their voices, her mom's and the deep voice which had to belong to Jeremy's father. Then there was her dad. Her feet were bare, and she stopped and caught her reflection in the glass of the wall oven, quickly running her fingers through her hair and tucking it behind her ears, then pulling on the edge of the dirty wine-stained cardigan to cover her thin T-shirt.

She took one step and then another until she could see the living room. Her mom and dad were standing, talking to Jeremy and his dad, and there was Jeremy, standing next to an older version of himself. Everyone was quiet, staring at her. As she took in Jeremy and the shiner and busted lip he now sported, she knew her brother was responsible, and for a second, she silently thanked him.

"Hi…" Boy, that was pathetic, but what did you say to the man who was the father of your child? He hadn't had a clue Brandon was his—until now.

"Tiffy, there are some things I guess we need to discuss," Jeremy said, and she didn't miss the way his father was watching her. Her mom and dad seemed to have figured out that something was off.

"Discuss…what is this about?" Flo finally said, looking from Tiffy to Jeremy's dad. Her dad, too, seemed at a loss.

"It seems that your son, Alex, is responsible for Jeremy's busted-up face," Tiffy said to her mom, stepping into the living room, where Brandon was holding up one of the big Tonka trucks and not saying a word, just watching everyone. What was it about kids? They seemed to have a sixth sense when something wasn't right and suddenly became so quiet.

"Mom, Dad, can you take Brandon into the bedroom? Brandon, go with Granny," she said, seeing the alarm on her mom's face.

Her dad, too, took in Brandon and then Tiffy. "You know what?" he said. "I think I'll stay. Flo…"

Her mom leaned down to Brandon after only a second of what appeared to be shock, which she'd never seen on her mother's face before, even when she'd told her she was pregnant. Flo said something to Brandon that had him putting down the truck and holding her hand as he jumped and skipped beside her down the hall in his dirty PJ bottoms.

Tiffy crossed her arms, feeling the tension ramp up, waiting until she heard her mom and Brandon at the far end of the house, likely in her parents' room. Then she turned back to Jeremy.

"You say Alex did that to your face?" her father said, confused. "Must've been something pretty serious that went down, as you boys have been friends forever." Her dad shoved his hands in the front of his jeans pocket, his multicolored short-sleeved shirt resting on the slight bulge of his stomach. Her dad wasn't a short man, but he also wasn't Jeremy or his dad's height.

"So why are you here?" Tiffy cut in before anyone could answer her dad. Of course, Jeremy gave nothing away as she did her best to look at him, the flicker of heat in his eyes, his amazing body, everything about him that had always reduced her to the woman who'd do anything to be with him. Except she was now stronger. She refused to be affected by this man. She wouldn't let him get under her skin.

He took a careful step toward her and then another until he was standing right in front of her. "You seriously need to ask that?" he said, staring right at her, and for a minute, all she could do was hold her breath as she waited, wondering what he'd say. "Is Brandon my son?"

There it was, and even though she'd been expecting this, she'd hoped that somehow he'd stay away.

CHAPTER
Nine

S
he was still shaking inside even though she was pretty sure everyone believed she was handling all of this rather calmly. She wasn't, because having Jeremy show up and actually demand to see his son and act as if she were in the wrong for not telling him wasn't sitting well with her at all.

She was still barefoot but was now in a loose pair of jeans and a slate green tank top as she stood in the laundry room, folding the last of the clothes she'd pulled from the dryer. Her hair was wet after the shower she'd taken after her dad had somehow managed to get Jeremy and his father out the door. He had gone with them. Where, she didn't have a clue.

There was a knock on the doorframe, and she turned to see her mom standing there, her expression oddly amused.

"Wow, you really know how to yank the rug out from under everyone," Flo said. "Just got off the phone with your dad, who is right now out at the Friessen ranch. He managed to talk down the sheriff, who wanted to drag your brother into the station and sit him in a cell because he tried to run Jeremy down and then proceeded to beat the hell out of the boy while muttering nonstop about how he was going to kill him. Your brother dug himself into a mess, but your dad managed to convince the sheriff it was just his temper and the shock of learning his best friend had broken the cardinal rule of the bro code and touched his sister." Her mom was actually smiling now, though Tiffy was anything but amused.

"Mom, how can you and Dad make it sound as if it's nothing? I still can't believe Alex took off and did what he did, and then telling Jeremy about Brandon… He had no right. Alex needs to get his out-of-control temper together. Going off like he did and pulling that stupid-ass shit…" She wanted to slug him for setting in motion what he had without thinking of the consequences for Tiffy and her son. She wondered when he would learn that it did no good to act on pure emotion. She was still shaking her head as she folded the last of her son's shirts and then lifted the pile. She went to step out of the laundry room, but her mom was blocking the door.

"Alex is just a little high spirited, but his intentions were good. Not to worry, your dad will have a talk with him, and he'll come around. But more to the point and the real issue, Jeremy is Brandon's father. Well, once I got past the shock, I can honestly say I didn't see that coming, Tiffy. When you told your father and me you were moving to your Aunt Rita's to finish your high school, that you were pregnant and it didn't matter who the father was because you were having the child and keeping it, and you figured it was better to go somewhere no one knew you because you didn't want to hear all the questions, you wanted to save your sanity and it was best to just up and move, new start, new beginning…pretty sure those were your exact

words, how you'd made your mind up, and we didn't stop
you. You've always been so headstrong, figuring things out,
planning in such detail that it drove your father and me
batty at times. You always were the exact opposite of your
brother. Where he acts on pure raw emotion, you on the
other hand are too logical, and neither is a good thing. You
need to live a little, Tiffy. Learn to let go."

Was she kidding? Maybe it was the expression on her
face that had her mother shaking her head and stepping
back into the kitchen, where a ham was sitting in a roaster.
There was a can of pineapple rings beside it, and her mom
pulled out a can opener and started opening it. Evidently,
Alex was going to be there for dinner, because they were
having ham.

"There's nothing wrong with being logical," Tiffy said,
noting the twitch of her mom's lip as she opened the can
of pineapple and dumped it into a bowl, then pulled a fork
from the drawer and laid the rings on the ham, covering it.

"There. That looks like something your father would
do, right?" Flo appeared to be thinking, and Tiffy
wondered why she was trying to cook, since she was a
disaster in the kitchen.

"Dad would add cloves as well," she said and took in
the frown on her mom's face as she swept her hand in the
air, then turned on the wall oven behind her and slid the
ham in.

"Well, I'm not fiddling with it," Flo said. "I'm sure this
will be just fine. Your dad will be home soon, and he can
fix it. Just for the record, Tiffy, being too logical is just as
wrong as being too emotional. You and Alex are sitting at
opposite ends of the spectrum. You need to find a nice
balance in the middle. The two of you together make the
perfect child. Just tell yourself, Tiffy, you don't need to be
too serious about everything. You've always had this need

to plan out everything, and your brother is about flying by the seat of his pants. You should try a little of that. It would lighten you up a bit."

She'd forgotten how her mom could be, and for a second she didn't have a clue what to say. At the same time, she was speechless that her mom was actually encouraging reckless behavior. "You know what, Mom? That was what created this situation—you know, that reckless behavior that got me knocked up with Brandon to begin with?" she said, seeing the toys scattered everywhere and knowing her mom had tucked Brandon into their bed, where he was fast asleep.

"Oh, there you go, being too hard on yourself," Flo said. "It's done. You can't go back, and now we have this amazing grandson who we just adore, and he has a father, another family. You can't keep him from his father, so you need to fix this. The Friessens are nice people, and coming here the way they did says a lot. Jeremy…you just have this way about you sometimes. You know how to push a boy's buttons. Ease up a bit."

Was she serious? Tiffy held the still warm clothes as her mom walked around the island and slid her hand over her shoulder, turning her. Then she somehow had her walking down the hall.

"You go on and put on something nice, because you need to go and have a talk with Jeremy, just you and him. Work it out. Work something out, Tiffy. This isn't just about you anymore," Flo said, patting her back as she gave her a shove into her old room, where the futon was stacked with fresh clean sheets and blankets and her suitcase was open on the floor. That was the only place she could put her and Brandon's clothes, since there wasn't even a dresser left in the room to unpack. "You need to go see Jeremy. Take my car, drive on out there—oh, and…" Her mom stepped back in the doorway, her expression happy and free of any stress. "You'll take Brandon with you, because now that it's out in the open and everyone knows, it's time Brandon met his father. Tell him he has a father."

She just stared at her mom. "What, no! Mom, seriously, I'm not taking Brandon with me. I'm not doing that. Jeremy is reckless, a chick magnet, a player, irresponsible…" She noted the way her mom crossed her arms and lifted a brow, which had her stopping and letting out a breath, as she could feel her blood pressure spiking again. "Jeremy is definitely not the kind of guy who is father material," she finally said and dropped the clothes onto the futon. "I do not want my son getting hurt."

Her mom's mouth made an O. "I see," she said. "This is about you being hurt and slighted. Okay, well, that makes perfect sense. By all means, cut Jeremy out of your son's life and keep him away from him. Except there's one little problem with that entire concept. Jeremy has insisted on seeing his son. He knows about him now, and from the impression I have of his father, his family, they aren't the kind to just walk away.

"Let's just say, playing devil's advocate," she continued, "that you manage to keep Jeremy away from Brandon. How much time is going to go by until Brandon starts asking about his father? Have you thought about that? Because he will, and no matter how much you want to wish it away and keep Jeremy away, Brandon is going to want to get to know his father. How do you think he'll feel when he finds out, because he will, that his father made every attempt to get to know him, wanted a relationship with him, yet his mother, you, wouldn't allow it?" Her mom again raised her brows, seriousness in her astute blue eyes. She didn't have to raise her voice for Tiffy to get where this was going.

"Fine, you win, but I'm not taking Brandon." She lifted her hand before her mom could say a word. "I'll go talk to Jeremy, but no promises."

An odd smile touched her mom's lips. "That's great. Now put on something nice—and low cut," her mom added as she stepped out of the room.

Tiffy just stared at the empty doorway, feeling for a second as if her mom had just maneuvered her into doing exactly what she'd wanted. But then, as good a negotiator as her dad was, her mom had always been just that much better. People never realized until they were walking away that Flo had just managed to get them to do everything she wanted, and then some.

Only Tiffy had no intention of putting on anything low cut or sexy.

CHAPTER

Ten

L aura had scrubbed the same spot on the kitchen
island five times. Jeremy was positive she was now
stripping off whatever veneer covered the granite
top, and she'd said not one word to him since he'd walked
into the house with his dad to find that the sheriff had Alex
parked in a chair, the very same chair he was sitting in now
that Alex, Wayne, and the sheriff had left.

His dad was leaning against the counter, saying something to his mom. It wasn't so much the fact that she'd said
nothing to Jeremy that worried him. It was how quiet she'd
become. She wasn't angry, because that would've been
something he could handle. He'd never seen his mom this
upset before. She was so quiet, as if her anger had an edge
of hurt to it, and he didn't really understand why she
would feel that way. After all, he was her son.

His dad glanced back to him, and he knew he was the
subject of their discussion. Correction, his dad was doing
all the talking while his mom scrubbed everything, her
mouth tightly closed. It didn't take a rocket scientist to
figure out the problem from where he sat, his back to the

window, watching his parents, feeling the emotion of the moment.

He was at a loss. Wayne Cahill had convinced everyone that clearer heads now prevailed, and now that all this nonsense was out in the open, no one would be killing anyone. He had even laughed as he said it. Alex had simply stared down Jeremy from across the room and given the obligatory nod, but his eyes said that he'd just as soon punch him in the face and kick his ass again. Alex would never forget what he'd done, and their friendship was over.

Then there was the date he was supposed to have been going on tonight. He didn't need to hear a word to know there wasn't a snowball's chance in hell of that happening now, even though he'd never been interested in going in the first place. It made him sick to think of the hate in his friend's eyes as he rested his cell phone on the table. He turned over the screen when he heard a ding.

Hey there boss, got Dorothy's message you're in charge while she's gone. Like that's so totally awesome!! Is there anything you need me to do? Cady 😊

He just stared at the message, knowing he should've stopped in already. He still needed to, but with everything, he just couldn't stop remembering what Dorothy had said about Cady loving him from afar. He squeezed his phone, seeing the dots flashing that let him know she was texting again.

I'm off at five. But could stay later? Just let me know…give me a call. I'll be waiting…

He couldn't deal with this right now. Who was closing? Ruth, maybe.

No, busy with my family! Who's closing? he said, then hit send and waited, knowing he was being rude, but at this point he didn't care. The last thing he wanted or needed right now was any unwanted female attention.

Ruth is closing. But again I can stay…

No, go at 5. Ruth will close. Text me if any problems. He hit send again and immediately got another text back.

You bet boss, have a great night with your family. 😊 😊

He took in the two smiley faces and put down his phone, feeling unusually creeped out, likely because he didn't have a clue what Cady was thinking. Good grief, she was, like, seventeen. He thought so, anyway.

Then there was the memory of Tiffy, who had stared at him as if he were something she was trying to wipe from the bottom of her foot. He pressed his thumb and fore-finger to the bridge of his nose, feeling the ache from Alex's fist.

When he pulled his hand away, he realized his mom was there with a sponge, and she just stood there with a look in her eyes that let him know how unhappy she was with him. He heard a knock at the door, but his mom didn't pull her gaze from his.

"Tiffy's here," he heard his dad call out, and he went to get up.

"Sit down," Laura said in a tone he'd never heard before. He didn't hesitate, taking in the fire that simmered in her green eyes, letting him know she wouldn't hesitate to step in and smack him up the backside of the head. That was something she'd never done before, but it seemed that today was a day of first times.

"Jeremy Friessen, you know you've done a lot of things over the years that I've had to chalk up to youthful mistakes, as your father put it—but this…this is just beyond."

"Mom," he started, but she'd tossed the sponge onto the table and snapped the flat of her hand in the air.

"No, you stop right now and you listen to me, you hear me? There's no talking your way out of this. You screwed up, big time, and there's a little boy out there, your son, our grandson, with his mother, alone." His mom rested her palms on the table, leaning in, and he took in the fact that despite how tiny she was, it seemed as if she could take on an entire army with her anger. He said nothing, knowing she had more to say.

"She was fifteen years old, and you didn't think for a second about how wrong that was."

Maybe his dad had forgotten to fill his mom in on how Tiffy had never told him about being pregnant. "You know, Mom, you don't have all the facts. You can't be angry at me for something I didn't know about."

His mom stood straight and then stepped around the table until she was standing right in front of him. He swallowed, because this wasn't his friendly nice mom who made sure everyone got along. "Facts? You mean *your* facts. There is only one fact here, Jeremy. You slept with her— no, scratch that. You had sex with your best friend's sister. Talk about having no respect for boundaries. Whatever you want to say to explain this away, I'm not really sure I want to hear your side."

His dad appeared in his line of sight. When his gaze drifted to his mom, he could see such love there and something else that was so protective. "Laura," Andy said, stepping in closer, "Jeremy needs to go talk with Tiffy."

His mom didn't move, only turned to his dad. Her hand was on her hip, and then she nodded and stepped back. There was nothing in her expression that eased at all, and he wasn't sure whether it was safe to get up. His dad didn't try to touch her, to reach out, nothing, and that was so unlike him. Laura just strode past him, and Andy let her keep walking before dragging his icy blue eyes back to Jeremy.

"You need to go talk to that girl in there," he said and

gestured with his thumb behind him. "She's in the living room, likely now getting some support from your mom. Word of advice, keep that temper of yours in check. Snapping and losing it the way you did earlier today isn't going to fix this."

So now his dad was against him, too. "You were there," Jeremy said. "What am I supposed to say? I'm starting to wonder how I'm supposed to fix this when she wants nothing to do with me. Seriously, did you hear the way she talked about me?"

She'd made him sound like a world-class jerk. It had horrified him, the way she'd portrayed him, even though he'd done what she'd said. It hadn't been like that, though. He'd been dating around, screwing his way through school. It was what he did, and he'd never been anything but totally one hundred percent up front with every girl he'd taken out. It was purely sex, nothing more. Everyone had been onboard except, apparently, Tiffy, who'd been knocked up from a one-time romp even though he'd worn a condom.

There wasn't an ounce of sympathy in his dad's expression, and his best friend now despised the ground he walked on.

"I was there, Jeremy, and heard it all," Andy said, "but let me point out that for whatever reason, she didn't believe you'd stand by her, likely because you were moving from one girl to the next. You're a player, and she's angry. It's understandable from your actions that she'd think you wouldn't have cared. At the same time, she did make it sound as if you'd slept with the entire county. I knew you weren't a saint, and I understand, but at the same time… have you asked yourself how many other kids you may have out there, running around? That kind of careless lifestyle comes with a cost, you know."

He just blinked, not sure if his dad was trying to mess with him or if he was serious. His throat closed up, and he squeezed his fists, feeling the dampness in his palms.

"You used protection, but evidently it didn't work," Andy said. He tapped the table and gestured as Jeremy stood up with an awful feeling in the pit of his stomach. He felt his dad's hand slip over his shoulder and squeeze. "You look like you're going to pass out."

Jeremy pulled in a breath and then another. Not once in his life had he ever been terrified of anything, but right now he was scared shitless that he wouldn't be able to figure this out. He pulled in another breath and made a face, and then his dad gestured with his chin to get moving.

"And your mom," Andy said. "You're going to need to make this right with her."

Jeremy didn't have a clue what to say, so he took that as his cue to walk out of the kitchen and face yet another person who was angry with him. No words were necessary, so he took a step and then another, feeling the heat of his dad behind him. Then he took in the living room and how quiet the house was. Sarah, Zach, Gabriel, where were they? Not here, thankfully.

There she was, Tiffy, her dark hair past her shoulders, wearing a teal shirt and faded blue jeans that hung low. She was standing in the middle of the living room with his mom, who had her hand on her shoulder and was saying something to her. Then they both looked his way as if he were an unwelcome guest.

"Hi" was all he managed to get out. Then his mom stepped away and started toward him. He wasn't sure she was going to stop until she stood right in front of him, lifted her hand, and touched his chin, taking in his face before shaking her head.

"We'll be outside," Laura said, and he watched as she

and Andy stepped out the screen door and down the steps, giving them some privacy.

"Your mom is nice," Tiffy said. "She asked to see Brandon. Your dad mentioned it, as well." She was holding her elbows, her arms wrapped around her, and she appeared uneasy. He wasn't sure what to make of it.

He just nodded and shifted his gaze to the open door his parents had walked through. "Tiffy, since we're now talking about what we should have talked about to begin with…well, you're here. Can't say I expected that after what happened earlier."

She didn't even nod, just stared at him, her eyes a mesmerizing shade of blue. They were a deeper shade than her brother's, and he remembered now looking into them. They held a light that separated her from anyone he'd ever met. They were what had drawn him to her to begin with, along with her smile, her confidence, her ability to be who she was and not pretend she was someone else— but that had been three years ago.

She pulled in a breath. "Let's just say that while I haven't gotten past everything by any means, Jeremy, I'm here to talk, since my brother put two and two together this morning and then decided to lose it, and now you know." She gestured with the flat of her hand, and he didn't understand why it seemed she was trying to keep him out of her life, out of his son's life.

"Yes, I know now," he said, "and since we're talking, answer me this, because no matter how I try to understand what happened, what you did, I'm at a loss. Why…?" He gestured to her. "I mean, I get the fact that you think I would have just walked away. You were pregnant…and before you go on and on again with a bunch of excuses about how I hooked up with others after, remember there was no us, only sex at the lake, and you walked away just as much as I did. Then you decided that I somehow didn't have a right to know?"

This was everything he shouldn't be saying, but at the same time, he realized she'd been making excuses for not telling him. Maybe he should've been the one who was angry, not her. He took in the way her chest rose, but she didn't pull her gaze from him. She was so frickin' strong, and he couldn't remember her having tested him like this.

"You mean to tell me if I told you I was pregnant, you'd have…what?" she said, really looking at him.

He couldn't shake the fact that this felt like a test, and he didn't know how to answer. "You want me to tell you what I would've done back then if you'd told me?" He knew he was stalling as she nodded, the tough chick who seemed to be able to see inside him, and he wondered if she expected him to lie. "Honestly, I don't know what I would have done, but you never gave me the chance to do anything. Knowing now that Brandon is mine—and he is, right?"

There he went again. She narrowed her eyes and her face flushed, but he remembered what his dad had said before.

"So you think I was doing what you were doing," she said, "hopping from one guy to the next? No, I can assure you, Jeremy, there was only you. I'm evidently not made with the same lack of respect and such a low moral code. It would be easier to say he's not yours. Then you wouldn't be in our life, and all of this would be moot. I could be on my way and never hear from you again." She pulled a breath in, and he took in the way her chest rose, the way the shirt she was wearing clung to her breasts, the perfect roundness. She was so tiny, only a little taller than his mom, but she had such slim curves in all the right places.

He also couldn't get past the fact that he was pretty sure she'd just made another dig at his character.

"So you'd like a DNA test?" she said. "Because really, I'd just as soon walk away and give you a pass—"

"Enough," he said. He leaned in, feeling again how she seemed to know how to push every one of his buttons. "I know he's mine. He has my eyes, the resemblance is there, and stop with the slights, Tiffy. Whatever happened, I never kept something from you the way you have from me."

She pursed her lips and pulled in another breath, and his eyes dropped again to the rise of her breasts. Damn, he needed to stop that, so he dragged his hand across his chin as she glanced to the side. He knew his mistake when the sharp pain bit in his jaw again. He must have made a face, as Tiffy was staring at him, and he thought there was sympathy there.

"So how do you want this to work, then?" she said. "You don't want a DNA test, but we should get one, have it done and over with, because I don't want this to be something you use against me down the road, throwing it in my face that I may have been two-timing you and you're not even sure he's yours." She didn't offer anything else.

He just stared, because there was something appealing about being sure, but she was making him sound like an asshole. He just shook his head. "Seriously?" was all he could say. "I know he's mine."

"Fine," she snapped. "So you want to see Brandon."

"Of course I do. I'm his father."

She nodded, her lips firmed. "He doesn't know about you, so I'll need to tell him, but hear me on this, Jeremy: You want to be in his life, you're in it. You be responsible. No fucking off on him or bringing your lifestyle around him. You don't get to decide one day that he's too much work or responsibility, because being a parent means being there…"

The squeak of the door had her stopping and him turning to see his mom and dad. He wondered whether they'd heard. The expressions on their faces told him they'd heard everything.

"He's our grandson, Tiffy," Andy said. "We have a right to know him, and he has a right to know us."

His mom, though, looked from him to Tiffy, and he wasn't sure what she was thinking. Then the phone started ringing, and Laura walked into the kitchen. He heard her answer it.

"Fine." Tiffy lifted her hands as if surrendering. "I'll bring him by so you can meet him, but first I'll need to tell him about you, because he doesn't know you exist." She was looking at Jeremy again.

"Great," he said, "but when you tell him, I want to be there."

CHAPTER
Eleven

There was something about the way this was all unfolding that was outside Tiffy's comfort zone. It was as if some outside force had stepped in and taken her carefully orchestrated plan, ripped it up, and tossed it all out the window, and there wasn't a damn thing she could do about it.

She listened to the voices from the living room, her mom and Laura. When she lifted her head, she could see them talking as if they were long-lost friends. It was freaking ridiculous, and what was she doing but standing at the kitchen island, mashing potatoes?

"Don't forget the butter, Tiffy," Wayne said. His thinning dark hair was freshly colored to hide all the gray, she knew, and the smile he had for everyone seemed to ease a lot of the tension in the house.

She took in her mom and Laura again, laughing now, then turned to the sliding glass door. Brandon was laughing in the back yard, and she wondered what he was doing with Jeremy. Everyone seemed so happy except her.

"And you're not getting enough of your arm in there,"

Wayne said. "Come on, you've really got to put some muscle in there and dig in, whip them up, or the potatoes will be all lumpy. You know what? Give me that masher, I'll do it, because you need to go outside and bite the bullet, so to speak." Her dad took the potato masher from her hand. "Go. You've stalled long enough. You need to tell Brandon that young man out there is his father and this nice couple here, Laura and Andy, are his grandparents. He deserves to know, and you're making this painful for everyone with all this stalling. I'll finish up dinner, and then we can all sit down to a nice meal as one big family."

Her dad made it sound as if it was a trivial thing, but this entire situation was life-changing, and she could feel her stomach knot again just as she heard the footsteps and the door opening and then slamming shut. Alex. The way he walked in, it seemed as if something else had just gone wrong. He pulled open the fridge, and she exchanged a glance with her dad, who was wearing a bib-style apron over his black short-sleeved shirt.

"Everything all right there, Alex?" Wayne said as her brother held the plastic milk carton and unscrewed the cap, then lifted it to his mouth to chug. Tiffy reached for the jug and pulled it away.

"If you don't mind using a glass," she snapped. "We're all drinking that milk, and I'd just as soon not have your backwash in there." She screwed the cap back on, taking in the face her brother made as he glanced out the window, likely seeing Jeremy, and then over to her mom and Laura. Brandon really did have Laura's eyes, Jeremy's eyes. The color was so distinct, and then there was his face, his hair, and something else that said he was the spitting image in personality, too, she thought.

"So why are they here?" Her brother sounded accusing as he lifted his hand and swept it to the window as if they were unwelcome neighbors and everyone was just waiting for them to leave. He was now leaning against the counter, and Tiffy gave her dad all her attention, wondering what he'd say.

"Yeah, Dad, why are they all here again?" she said. "Oh, yeah, because Mom phoned Laura and invited all of them over for dinner tonight."

While she'd been at the Friessen ranch, trying to make nice with Jeremy, Flo had called and spoken to Laura before she could come up with a plan about how to tell Brandon that Jeremy was his father. Yup, they'd had her out the door right away and had followed her into town, and they'd been there ever since. She still needed to tell Brandon, which was likely where the sick feeling she could feel growing in her stomach came from.

"It's only right," Wayne said. "We should get to know the Friessens, and having dinner together is the best way. They are Brandon's family, too, so that makes us all family. Sitting together over a meal, talking as the civilized human beings that we are, is the best way to build something good and amicable. Now, Tiffy, you've stalled long enough. Go tell Brandon, and then dinner will be on the table in five minutes. Alex, you can set the table."

Wayne was still holding the masher, and he took the milk jug from Tiffy and poured some in the potatoes. She just shook her head and strode over to the sliding glass door before stepping out sock-footed onto the deck, seeing Andy Friessen sitting in one of the six patio chairs, watching Jeremy toss a plastic ball to Brandon, who tried to hit it with a big plastic baseball bat. It was one of the many toys her parents had bought for him.

It was still nice out, but she could feel the chill in the air as the sun slipped lower in the sky. It was the late fall air. She realized Andy was watching her.

"Come sit down," he said, gesturing to one of the chairs.

"I need to tell Brandon about Jeremy. Looks like he's having fun." She knew she was stalling and could feel her feet dig in. Her legs didn't want to move. She didn't know why she was so nervous, maybe because she'd never expected to have Jeremy in her life. It was unsettling. He was the guy everyone wanted, and she wasn't about to be that girl with that kind of guy.

She heard the chair scrape back, and Andy stood up. She had to look up since he was so tall, just like his son, an older version of Jeremy. She wondered if there were any other traits he'd gotten from his father. Andy was all about his family, though, whereas Jeremy was all about having fun. She'd heard that enough times from Alex.

"He's a great kid, Tiffy," Andy said. "You did that alone?"

She could hear her son laughing and playing and jumping, and she wasn't sure what to make of the way Andy was staring down at her.

"I had my aunt, my mom's sister," she replied. "I went and stayed with her, you know, a new start, a new beginning, so I wouldn't have to answer a thousand questions from everyone. It worked well."

For a time, she thought, but Rita wasn't her mom. She was a free spirit multiplied by one hundred, never the doting aunt, even though she always had a smile for everyone. So yes, she'd done it alone with Brandon, but it wasn't as he was making it out to be, because she'd never felt as if she had no one.

"I had options," she finally said, and that was why she'd decided one day to move back to Columbia Falls.

Andy motioned to his son, and Jeremy said something to Brandon, and they were both coming her way.

"Mommy, I'm hungry!" Brandon shouted and raced over to her. He jumped up, wrapped his arms around her legs, and was standing on her feet, still wearing the same dirty pajama bottoms, his dark hair messy. As she stared down at him, seeing clearly the resemblance between son, father, and grandfather, she swallowed and couldn't look up.

"Well, Grandpa has dinner almost ready, but first I need to tell you something." She rested her hand on his head. God, this was painful. She was making it painful!

"Yeah!" he said, all smiles and jumping on her foot as he held her leg. She wondered how much he'd really understand of what she was about to say.

"You know how it was always just you and me and Aunt Rita, and then we came back here to stay with your grandma and grandpa and Uncle Alex? Well, I didn't tell you about your daddy."

He frowned and had an odd look on his face. "You said I didn't need one because I had you."

She didn't need to look up to know Jeremy was likely ready to add a word or two to that. "Well, that's true, I did say that—but Jeremy here is your dad, and he wants to get to know you," she said.

Jeremy was shaking his head at her, likely in disbelief. She just shrugged as her son let go of her legs and was staring up at Jeremy, hopping up and down.

"You're my dad? Yeah!" he said. So much for him being upset.

"And that makes me your other grandpa," Andy said, "and the nice lady in there with your grandma is Jeremy's mom, so you know what that makes her?"

Tiffy watched as Andy squatted down to her son, his face lit up with a smile. He really was a handsome man, with a natural charm just like his son's. They had the same killer smile.

"My granny!" Brandon was so excited and jumping up and down again, and Andy was now laughing.

"That's right, she is, so how about you come with me inside, because she's been dying to get her hands on you, and we'll leave your mommy and daddy out here to talk?"

Andy lifted Brandon and tossed him over his shoulder.

"Bye, Mommy! Bye, Daddy!" Brandon laughed and waved, and she couldn't believe how happy he was and how none of this seemed a big deal to him. But then, he was only two, and she hadn't had a chance to totally screw him up yet, especially considering his father lacked the moral compass a great role model should have. That was what she remembered. Maybe that was why she wanted nothing more than to follow Brandon into the house and just ignore Jeremy. She could do it. She knew she could.

"Wow, you really said that to Brandon, that it was just you and him and he doesn't need a father? I guess we've already established how little you think of me," Jeremy said, and she just stared at him—his broad shoulders, his light T-shirt pulled across his impressive chest, and she had to fight the urge to let her eyes lower and take in all of him. After all this time, she thought she'd exorcised Jeremy Friessen out of her. He was so close, and she could smell him. He'd always smelled so good. Even his busted lip and the bruising on his jaw, his eye, his nose didn't take away from how handsome he was. He was eye candy.

"So can I be brutally honest here?" she said and took in the way a smile touched his lips. His eyes sparked, and she'd have been a fool to miss the warning that she was pushing him into a corner and she might not like how he reacted.

"By all means, Tiffy. Let's hear it." He leaned in, and

she picked up the edge to his anger. If she was smart, she'd step back, even though she wouldn't admit to anyone that this sparring of wills excited her. He was interesting in a way he shouldn't be.

"You're not father material," she said. "Why, just this morning, before all of this and you finding out about Brandon, you were about to help my brother out with Sky's cousin, and then she'd be just another notch on your considerably vast bedpost. I have to wonder if you remember the names of every girl you've slept with. I can't help wondering if maybe I'm not alone. I mean, how many other little Jeremy Friessens could be running around out there? And here you are—"

He lifted his hand and sliced it in the air. "Enough already. I'm a guy, okay? I never said I was a saint, but you're not painting an accurate picture, Tiffy. You must think I'm pretty shallow if you think I can't remember the names of every woman I've slept with. That's not true. As for having another kid out there, the only way that would happen is if there was another broad like you who felt the need to keep it a secret and take off. Don't forget, I wore a condom. How it happened with you is beyond me."

She could see from his fisted hands that she was pushing every one of his buttons. *Good!* She was tempted to call him out on whether he knew every woman's name, but if she did, the thought of hearing them was something she knew she wouldn't be able to stand.

"Okay, this is getting us nowhere," she said. "I've said my peace, so you know how I feel. Don't fuck it up, Jeremy —and one other ground rule: No women around my son." She pulled her arms across her chest and wasn't sure what to make of his expression.

"That goes two ways, baby," he replied, leaning in, his arms also crossed. "No guys around my kid."

"Okay, you two!" Wayne called, appearing in the door-way. "Dinner is ready. Come in, and let's save the rest of this for another time."

She turned to Jeremy, wanting to say she'd changed her mind, but her dad swept his hand inside.

"Come on, now," he said.

Jeremy wasn't the happy, fun, charming guy she remembered. Who he was now was moody, difficult, and too damn good looking—and the father of her child. There was something about this kind of forever with a man that didn't quite sit right with her.

"Tiffy…" Jeremy lifted his hand, and she wondered whether he was going to touch her back. Then he gestured to her dad, and instead of arguing, she lifted her chin and started walking into the house, to a dinner with two fami-lies she'd never expected to find sitting around the same table.

CHAPTER
Twelve

He was seated at one end of the bench, and Tiffy was at the other end, Brandon in between them at the large oval table. He was sure the food was good as he took in the fluffy whipped potatoes, ham, baby carrots, and salad, his senses on overload. He was unable to taste anything, though, and only vaguely heard the conversation around him as his son fidgeted beside him, using his hands over his fork.

"Come on, Brandon," Tiffy said. "Use your fork like a big boy. You're not a baby anymore. Up on your knees. Sit up, eat your dinner, stop playing."

He had listened to the battle of wills between mother and son, adding, "Listen to your mother, and try the ham." Brandon had complained he didn't like it and it was too chewy.

Then there was Alex, who steadily shoved food in his mouth, all the while looking as if it wouldn't be beyond him to launch himself across the table and finish what he'd started just that morning. Jeremy noticed the bruising on his fists. *Good!*

"Alex, I thought you had a date with Sky tonight," said Flo, who reached out and tapped his shoulder from where she sat beside him. That was the only time Alex pulled his gaze away from Jeremy.

"Nope," he said. "Had to cancel, since the date for her cousin turned out to be a deadbeat loser who can't be trusted." He swung his gaze back to Jeremy, and it landed with a punch. He squeezed his fork.

"What's a deadbeat?" Brandon asked in his innocent way, and Jeremy put down his fork, his hand on his son's lower back and his thin T-shirt. He wondered why Tiffy was letting him run around in just PJ bottoms this late in the day.

"It's just your uncle's limited vocabulary," Jeremy said. "Don't pay him any mind," he added, and he didn't miss the way his dad was watching Alex, too.

"You know what I meant," Alex snapped and pointed his knife straight out at Jeremy before resuming cutting into his ham and shoving a big chunk into his mouth.

"Okay, Alex, enough already," Tiffy said. "If you forget, your very impressionable young nephew isn't supposed to be the mature one here. Jeremy is his father and intends to get to know him, so how about giving us all a break with this?" Tiffy was leaning in and gestured with her fork across the table to Alex.

"Fine, got it," Alex snapped and shoved another piece of ham in his mouth. His cheeks puffed out, and Jeremy didn't think he'd ever give him a pass. Could he blame him? If it had been Alex with Chelsea… He didn't want to go there.

"So I was thinking about Brandon coming out to the ranch, maybe for a sleepover," Laura said. "Would love to have a chance to spoil him, and he could meet the rest of the family." She hadn't been able to resist giving a smile to his son, but then she looked Jeremy's way, and there it was again, something that said she still had something more to say to him.

Great! Still in my mom's bad books.

"Well, I'm not sure about that…" Tiffy started.

"I think it's a great idea—and a must," Jeremy said. "Hey, bud, what do you think about spending the night with me and my family at our ranch? It's huge, and we have horses and cattle, and tomorrow I can show you the horses, put you on a pony…"

"Uh, no," Tiffy said, cutting him off, leaning around her son.

"Yeah, yeah! A pony!" Brandon shouted and launched himself into Jeremy's arms, and Jeremy lifted him and held him, his son, in his lap. Brandon was so happy, and he was squeezing Jeremy's arm.

"No horses or ponies," Tiffy said. "I'm not kidding. There's no way they're safe, and Brandon is only two. You're not putting him on one."

He'd never seen Tiffy so upset, and even Brandon became quiet.

"You don't think horses are safe?" Andy asked.

Laura, meanwhile, had such sympathy in her eyes for Tiffy, who he could see was wound up so tense he thought she'd lose it if he touched her, if anyone touched her.

"You know what?" Tiffy said. "I get that you're comfortable with your life around horses and have the confidence to ride them and be okay with getting thrown and hurt and stomped on, but not Brandon. He's too young, and I'm his mother, and I said no." She actually took her napkin and tossed it on her half-eaten dinner, then slid out from the bench and stood, taking them all in before letting her gaze land on his parents. "I get that you want to see Brandon, to get to know him, but a sleepover is just too soon. And the horses…no, no, not ever. Excuse me, everyone," she said and walked away down the hall, and he heard a door close.

Like, what the hell was that?

Alex was no longer staring at him as if he wanted to kill him but was looking at his parents, at their expressions, which said there was something more to the situation. Then Jeremy took in Brandon, who looked as if he was going to cry.

"Hey, hey there, Brandon, it's okay," he said. His son was so quiet, bunching his shirt in his tiny fist. His other arm was around Jeremy's arm, holding him against him.

"I guess she's never gotten over it," Alex said to his parents.

"Over what?" Jeremy asked.

Flo shrugged, and Alex dragged his gaze back to Jeremy.

"She was thrown by a temperamental horse she had no business being on, and her foot caught in the stirrup," Wayne said, sitting up straighter. This was the first time Jeremy had seen him look so serious. "She was dragged about a thousand yards upside down before she got her foot free."

"How bad was she hurt?" Laura asked.

Jeremy just stared at his friend, who was looking from him to Brandon, whom he was still holding.

"Just scrapes and bruises, and she was stiff for a week," Flo said. "I don't think she could move without wincing for a few days. She was lucky that's all that happened. Don't know what she was thinking, getting on that horse."

Alex was now staring at him. "It was a dare," he said and tapped the table with his fingers, dropping his gaze.

Jeremy leaned closer and held his son tighter. "From

who, you?" he snarled. He didn't need to look over to his dad to know he was getting ready to step in.

Alex made a face. "No, some friend of hers, Stephanie, had a stable of horses. She did all that show jumping. High-spirited Arabians, thoroughbreds, the kind no one has any business being on unless they're super confident and super good with horses. Stephanie dared her, saying she was too chicken. That was the first and last time I've ever seen her succumb to taunting. Next thing, she was getting on that horse. She'd barely sat in the saddle when it took off…" Alex shook his head.

Jeremy didn't know what to say, wondering why anyone would be that cruel and careless as to stick someone who didn't know anything about a horse onto an animal that couldn't be handled easily. "And you were there?" he said accusingly. He just couldn't help it, wanting to shoot something back to Alex.

Alex made a face and a rude noise. "No, what kind of asshole do you take me for? Heard it from Kurt. Stephanie is his half sister. He was there. He saw it."

"And Tiffy's never gotten back on a horse again," Flo said. "What was she, ten, twelve?"

"Thirteen, Mom," Alex said before swinging his gaze back to Jeremy. "So, word of advice, don't push her on the horse thing." He pushed back his chair. "Great meal, Dad, but I got things to do."

Then Jeremy watched as Alex shot him a warning glare and then looked over to Brandon and grunted. He didn't offer another word as he too walked away down the hall, and he heard another door close.

His parents and Flo and Wayne picked back up in the conversation, and he took in Brandon, who was watching him with a tiny bit of worry, he thought. His son. He wondered why he'd never heard what had happened to Tiffy.

"Don't worry, Brandon," he said in a low voice. "I'll get your mommy to come around."

His little boy had a brilliant innocent smile, and Jeremy wondered what the difference would be between taming a wild untrained horse and taming Tiffy. One was far easier than the other, and it wasn't the horse.

CHAPTER
Thirteen

"So what are your plans today?" Flo said, settling a coffee down at the counter where Tiffy sat, combing through the paper and the help wanted section. She was showered, her hair wet and slicked back, wearing a thin floral robe her mom had left hanging in the bathroom, which she was grateful for, considering hers was likely still with the rest of her things back in Iowa.

She glanced up to see her mom dressed in blue jeans and a green and blue paisley blouse. She'd added makeup, nothing over the top, but it gave her a fresh look that let Tiffy know she was going somewhere today. Her dad had left at dawn for a standing engagement with three of his long-time golfing buddies. Then there was Alex, who she thought was at school, college, a place she'd given up any chance of going to after becoming a mother at sixteen.

"Getting a job," Tiffy replied. "I thought I would see what's available, then go in and see each one, drop off a resume. I plan to borrow your printer for a little bit. Hopefully I can find something above the pathetic minimum wage that seems to be offered everywhere, and I can start putting money away and get a place for me and Brandon, and Alex can have his gaming room back. Hopefully I'll be able to pay for groceries and everything else, and also buy a small used car, cheap. I can pay for all the incidentals, pay for daycare for Brandon when I work, and that'll still enable me to put away ten percent of my measly pay for a nest egg…"

Her mom held up the flat of her hand. "Stop. Seriously, Tiffy, stop trying to plan out your next twenty years." Flo gave her an exasperated look and then shook her head, pulling keys from her pocket. "You can take my car and use it whenever you want. Stop trying to manage everything. A job is a great idea, but you're already trying to get your own place for you and Brandon? Just stow away that idea for now. Your dad and I already told you home is home, and this is your home and Brandon's—and there are enough of us here that daycare should be at the bottom of your priorities. Even Alex can step in and spend time with his nephew. Then there are the Friessens, who want to spend time with him now. Between his grandparents, all of us, we can pick up most of the slack. No, there's more than enough family around."

She blinked as she lifted her coffee after circling five help wanted ads, one for serving staff at an eatery, one for a grocery store clerk, one for a hardware store clerk, one for an office assistant, and one for a fry cook at the Burger Bar. Wow, her options were exciting. *Not!* She wasn't so sure she wanted to start relying on others for her son, either.

"To be clear, Tiffy, you're back home now, living here, and you have other things that are a priority and far more important before all that."

"So what would those things be? Because I made a list and have prioritized it." She slid over her notebook with today's date and a clear outline of her plan and the steps she needed to take to achieve each goal. What could she have possibly forgotten? She did a quick scan of her list, feeling that anxiety of having overlooked something. "No, I have everything on here."

She glanced up to her mom, who had an odd look on her face. Her eyes danced with a mischief that said either she was messing with her or she was going to make her work for it. It was painful trying to figure out what her mom was thinking. It was just that odd twisty side of her mom that had always been far too easy-going and liked to toy with her need to be hyper organized and plan everything out. "Okay, what is it I've forgotten?" She scanned her list again and shifted her glance from her mom to the notebook.

"Oh, I'd say that Jeremy should be your priority."

She squeezed the pen she was holding and then set it down and closed up her notebook. "And how's that? From where I'm sitting, Jeremy is a nuisance who…"

"No, Tiffy." Her mom reached out and patted a hand over hers, which she'd fisted. "He's your priority right now because everything you've done for the past few years has been for Brandon. Jeremy is Brandon's father, and might I add…"

Tiffy pulled in a breath and went to interrupt, so Flo continued quickly.

"You kept Brandon's very existence from him, so you need to figure out where the two of you go as Brandon's parents. Put that at the top of your list along with your need to handle, decide, and outline your plan alone. Jeremy has a say in his son, and until he proves that he's a deadbeat, unfit womanizer, you need to cut him some slack and start talking." Her mom reached for her notebook and took it from her. "This list you've done, Tiffy…you need to start relaxing a bit. Yes, goals are great, and so are plans, but you're far too rigid in your thinking and always have been. You can't see outside your carefully drawn lines.

"Life isn't supposed to go as planned, and you need to be flexible enough to go with it and be able to catch that curve ball, because it doesn't always come as the expected line drive. You need to be okay with that. Jeremy is your curve ball, and as angry as you are at him for what he did way back when, there was no right in there with either of you, and the way he's here now and insisting to be part of Brandon's life along with Andy and Laura, you need to dial it back a bit and let them in. Be a big girl and get past everything you imagined could have happened but didn't. I know everything about Jeremy is freaking you out," her mom added, setting her notebook on the counter after shaking her head.

"Jeremy isn't freaking me out, Mom. I'm just not into someone so shallow, too good looking for his own good. He can have any woman he wants, and he knows it, with just a snap of his fingers…"

Her mom raised a brow, her expression amused. "Yup, terrified, you are, because the thought that anything could happen between you and that boy, or the thought of him suddenly giving you all his attention and wanting to build something with you, you can't handle it. I don't know why I didn't figure it out until now, but I saw it yesterday, and at dinner. You're throwing every roadblock you can his way, just waiting for him to disappear and become the dead-beat, irresponsible man he isn't."

What was her mom doing? She shook her head. "There's nothing between me and Jeremy. There never will be. He's not reliable," she stated, and this time her mom did laugh.

"Oh, Tiffy, there's everything between you and Jeremy, so go get dressed. Leave Brandon here, I've got him, and you can keep telling yourself Jeremy is going to up and walk, you can push and push, but he's not going anywhere. You have one hundred percent of his attention. I saw it, your dad saw it, and Alex…well, your brother isn't about to see it, but nevertheless, you need to make time for Jeremy. I can see you're having trouble with everything, so tell yourself it's for Brandon."

Her son came bouncing up the hall, awake, and raced into the kitchen naked.

"Brandon, clothes! Where is your pull-up?" She was off the stool, but her mom was already around the island, lifting Brandon, and he was giggling and laughing.

"You get yourself ready and do your job search thing, and then call you know who," her mom said before kissing Brandon, who had his legs wrapped around her. She walked back down the hall with him, and Tiffy touched her head as she thought about Jeremy, the what-ifs, that killer smile… *Hell, no! That's never going to happen.*

CHAPTER
Fourteen

"Hey, boss," Cady said. "Thought I'd stop in and see if you need anything or if you need me to pick up a shift, anything I can do to help out."

Jeremy looked up from where he stood behind the front counter and the pile of papers from all the orders that had come in. It was a paper nightmare, and he was determined to have a sit-down with Dorothy again when she got back about streamlining everything on a computer.

There was Cady, her dark hair hiked in a ponytail. Her dark-rimmed glasses kept slipping down her slender nose, and she continually pushed them back up to the bridge. She was a little on the plump side and wore an unflattering baggy T-shirt, but there it was: the smile he'd thought nothing of before.

"Ah, no, but thanks. Ruth's here, and it's been pretty slow," he added. It was another second before he noted the flash of disappointment. She was still standing there, and of course he remembered what Dot had said about her loving him from afar.

"Oh my God, what happened to your face?" she finally

said. The bruising made his face seem far worse than it felt, and he took in the horror and concern in her expression. She lifted her hand, and for a second he thought she was about to touch him. He stood straighter and stepped to the side so she couldn't reach him.

"Just an accident of sorts. No biggie, really. It looks worse than it is."

She was still staring at him, and he didn't miss how overly concerned she seemed, but then, that was the same overly feminine worry he'd gotten from Ruth when he'd walked in after his morning classes to be the responsible boss filling in for Dorothy.

"It looks like you were in a fight. Are you sure you're okay?"

He thought of his mom, who seemed to relish him suffering a little. His dad was right. He still needed to talk with her—and then there was Tiffy.

"Fine, Cady, so why are you here again?" he said. He really could be a prick without even trying, he noted, by the way her face flushed. "Sorry, just a long day. How's school going?" he threw in, and she seemed to recover, flashing another smile and leaning in closer on the counter.

"Oh, great, kind of slow and stuff. All those immature kids are still there, you know. Nothing's really changed since you were there." She was now leaning down on her elbows, and he just stared at her, wondering what the hell to say.

"I think it's so great that you're running everything," she continued. "Dot always said that running a business was in your blood. I'm going to college next year and decided to major in business. You can't go wrong with that, I figured. Isn't that what you're taking as well?" She was flashing him that smile again and giving him all her attention, and it seemed this could go on all day.

"It is," he said. "Good choice, business, but only if it interests you. At the same time, figure out what you want to do first, and don't forget to have some fun. Get that boyfriend of yours to take you out." He didn't know why he'd added that, but he was doing everything he could think of to steer her off of him. At one time, this conversation wouldn't have bothered him, but now, knowing what he did, it made him uncomfortable.

She shrugged. "I don't have a boyfriend, so I have time to go out."

He heard the ding of the door and thought someone had come in. He could hear Ruth saying hi and asking if whoever it was needed help with anything, and he stared at the hopeful look on Cady's face, one he wouldn't have picked up on before.

"Hey, boss, there's a lady here who wants to drop off her resume about that job Dorothy posted," Ruth said.

He clutched the invoices, glanced over Cady's head, and took in Ruth, tall and thin, walking his way. It took him a second to realize the lady in question was Tiffy, and the smile she'd pasted to her lips faded.

"Tiffy" was all he could say. He took in the paper she held and the fact that Ruth and Cady were staring at both of them.

"Jeremy, I didn't realize you worked here," Tiffy said, and he wondered whether the moment could become more awkward.

"Oh, you know Jeremy?" Ruth said. "He's actually in charge—well, while Dorothy is away."

Cady turned toward Tiffy but didn't relinquish her spot at the counter, and he didn't miss the way Tiffy's mouth had formed an O.

"Yeah, uh…" He held out his hand for the paper, not knowing what else to do, but she made no motion to hand it over. "Tiffy is the mother of my child. We're old friends, and…" He stopped talking at the shocked looks on Ruth and Cady's faces. Even Tiffy seemed thrown. "Tiffy, this is Ruth and Cady. They work here. Could you two give us a moment?"

They both nodded and moved to the other side of the store, though he was sure they were watching everything. He decided to step around the counter, closer to Tiffy, who glanced once over her shoulder to the door.

"You know what? I should go. I didn't realize you worked here…"

He reached for the paper she was holding and tugged until she let go, and he took in her resume and how neatly organized it was. "So you graduated high school in Iowa," he said. It was her history, a snapshot that told only a piece of the story.

"Yeah, I did, actually, online in one year. It's amazing how much time we wasted in high school. The actual courses take very little time—but again, Jeremy, this could never work, so I'll take that back and be on my way." She was touching the paper, and he took in her tiny hands, her short clipped nails, free of any polish or fancy anything, and her face, which was the perfect sort of round. He thought he could stare at her all day.

"It's irrelevant whether I'm working here or not. You need a job, Tiffy, and Dorothy is hiring. You worked at a bookstore and a garage?" He could see the dates and had already calculated that she'd have been pregnant at the bookstore, and the garage had been up until a few weeks ago. "You were pregnant then, and Brandon would've been a baby here. What did you do?"

He thought he saw her pull back as if getting ready to fight. "I still needed to work, pregnant or not, Jeremy. That's the way of the world. And for your information,

Brandon never went without. He was always looked after."

He didn't miss how defensive she was, and he folded up the paper and stuck it in his back pocket. "I'm not saying he wasn't, Tiffy. I mean, what exactly did you do at the bookstore and the garage?" Everything about where she'd been and done alone hit him, and he didn't expect to feel this sense of having abandoned her. A garage was not the kind of place he wanted her or his son.

"A bookstore is just that. I stocked shelves, pulled old books and ones that didn't sell. It was an easy part-time job when I was pregnant, and I socked money away. Although I didn't have to pay rent living with my aunt, I still needed to be able to cover costs for me, incidentals and stuff. The garage where I worked after Brandon was born was another part-time job. I could take him with me. It was a small place. I learned from one of the mechanics every-thing that can go wrong with a car, what to look for, how to change a timing belt, a flat, oil, typical stuff that just about everyone who owns a car completely overlooks. It was great until Brandon started walking, and then it was just too much, so Aunt Rita looked after him, and a neighbor, and another neighbor, and…." She stopped talking. There was so much more he wanted to know, like why she'd come back, why she hadn't told him about Brandon, and why she'd insisted on going it alone.

"And what, Tiffy? I have a lot of questions. No matter what you think of me, I care. You should've told me, you shouldn't have run, and you shouldn't have had to figure it out alone." He didn't pull his gaze from her and could feel Ruth and Cady too close in the background, so he slid his hand over Tiffy's shoulder and took in the way her eyes lingered there. "Just so you know, you can stop looking for a job," he said, and he felt her stiffen, ready to argue. "I mean it, Tiffy. You left me out of everything for too long—"

"I thank you, Jeremy, for your interest, but you can't tell me not to look for work. I have responsibilities and need to work to pay the bills, to buy a car, to rent a place, for Brandon's future, to put money away…"

"You're hired." He cut her off before she could finish, wondering what Dorothy would say.

For the first time, Tiffy was speechless.

CHAPTER
Fifteen

How had he managed to do it?

She was sitting in the passenger side of his pickup after he'd somehow hired her and convinced her to leave with him because they needed to talk about Brandon. At the same time, she took in the way his two coworkers watched him, eager to do anything for him, staring at him with puppy-dog eyes and longing from afar. She had to fight the urge to pull both aside and smack them upside the back of the head, tell them to wake up. After all, he was just a guy. A good-looking guy, yes, but that didn't give him godlike qualities and entitle him to have every woman drooling after him.

The one with glasses stared at her with unfriendliness, and the tall thin one with a wedding ring was watching her as if she were the subject of the town scandal. She'd yet to stand her ground and tell Jeremy no.

No to the job.

No to going anywhere with him.

No to letting him into her life so she had to watch him take up with whatever flavor of the month he was into. No, thank you. That was exactly what she wasn't about to do, becoming the girl who stood at the sidelines for whatever crumb he tossed her way.

"Where's Brandon?" he asked, turning onto the main road that led out to the subdivision where her parents' house was.

"With my mom. You know, Jeremy, you want to talk, fine, I get it, but my mom's car is parked at the hardware store. I'd just as soon not leave it there." Or rely on him for anything, even a ride.

He glanced her way, and there was something about the chemistry that seemed to ooze from him. She had to fight the urge to get sucked into it again. Hadn't that been what had put her in the situation she was in now? Jeremy was just too handsome, drop-dead gorgeous, with the body, the looks, the attitude, the charm, and the charisma, and he knew how to use it all. She had to force herself not to look at him.

"Your mom's car is fine. I'll take you back later to get it. Call your mom, tell her we're picking up Brandon."

She couldn't believe his arrogance. There was no asking. No, this was not going to happen. She crossed her arms, feeling the shoulder strap dig into her neck. "I thought you wanted to talk. Picking up Brandon isn't going to have us talking, and might I point out that we need to discuss arrangements? You want to get to know Brandon, fine, but we need a schedule that's mutually agreeable and doesn't conflict with Brandon's naps or with my family's lives. Then there's your social life," she added as she heard his phone ding. She took in the way he lifted his cell phone, glancing to the screen as he drove, and she wanted to add that he needed to leave his phone alone, as he was driving, and it was also the law.

"Save your breath," he said. "I got my answer. Brandon's at the ranch." He tossed his phone on the console beside him, and she knew her mouth was open from the shock.

"What did you say?" Damn her mom! What the hell had she done?

"Text from my mom," he replied. "Brandon is at the ranch. Your mom was just there and dropped him off. He's spending the night."

She vaguely heard herself wheeze and watched as Jeremy pulled a U-turn. She wanted to say this wasn't okay. She was stuck on Brandon being at the ranch, and no one had thought to ask her. "Damn it, Mom…" she said under her breath.

Jeremy watched her and then shook his head. "You're upset with your mom because…?" he asked.

What could she say, that she didn't want Jeremy or his family in her life, in Brandon's life? She shrugged. She didn't want to go back to that girl who'd watched Jeremy from afar and realized how meaningless their night at the lake had been. *No no no,* she wasn't going to have regrets, because then there would be no Brandon.

"You know what? Never mind. You wouldn't get it. Come to think of it, just turn around and take me back to your hardware store, and I'll pick up my mom's car." Then she'd drive out to the ranch, pick up Brandon, and have a word with her mom when she got home about boundaries and who was actually in charge.

"We need to talk, and don't think it's lost on me how you're still pushing to keep me away, as if you're deliberately trying to keep me from getting to know my son, and my parents too. They have a right to see their grandson, to get to know him, or are you about denying Brandon to all of us? Let me clear up one fact for you: I'm Brandon's father, and I never gave my rights away. I have no intention of walking away."

What was it about Jeremy that made her feel so much? This wasn't good. She fought the urge to touch her head so Jeremy couldn't figure out how under her skin he was. "So you believe he's yours," she said. What was she doing?

He slammed the brakes and pulled to the side of the road. She heard a horn blast.

"Jeremy! You crazy, reckless—"

"You fucking stop this bullshit right now, Tiffy. I'm so tired of this. Are you trying to say that he's not mine and that all of this is some big fucking game to you?" he snapped. She was pushing him the wrong way.

"No, he's yours, but I still think a DNA test is necessary."

"Oh, fuck the DNA test. I don't know why you keep pushing that shit when we can see he's mine. He looks just like me. I never took you for someone deceitful and dishonest. That's my son, mine, and you do not get to decide what's best for him or how I fit into his life or toy with me and dangle these doubts in front of me. I've heard enough. All I'm hearing is that you want to decide how and when anyone gets to know Brandon, but listen up, baby: The minute I fucked you and got you pregnant, I had a say. He's my kid, mine. So fuck you and this DNA bullshit. I'm tired of you tossing that in as if you think I'm about to hold out for something, ready to walk. You want a test? Fine, let's get the fucking test, but we both know how it's going to come out."

He lifted his hand and ran it over his thick dark hair, so perfectly messy. He was handsome even when he was angry. "And no more of this bullshit from you," he said. He was breathing hard, and his truck was still running.

She had seen a side of Jeremy she didn't know existed. She hadn't expected this.

"And you should have told me you were pregnant," he snapped before shoving the truck in drive, looking into his side mirror, and pulling back into traffic. "You never gave me a chance, and you took that away from me, his birth, Brandon as a baby, seeing his first step, his first tooth, his first word…"

"I'm sorry." She cut him off, the ache in her throat thickening. She could feel the heavy emotion in the truck. It wasn't passion but fire and angst that had settled between them, and she wondered how good this was. "I get it, but you need to understand something, Jeremy." She could feel her eyes burn, but there was no way she would allow him to get the best of her. She refused to be one of those women who cried at the drop of a hat or when something didn't work. It was downright embarrassing.

"Really, and what would that be, Tiffy? I'm dying to know, because everything you've said so far is just another excuse to explain away why you believed you didn't have to tell me. Let me be clear. You have no excuse, and there's nothing that I did or could have done that could justify you not telling me…"

"I fell in love with you." She shut her eyes, feeling the silence and hearing her heart pound long and loud in her ears. How could she say that?

He said nothing as he drove, and she couldn't make herself look his way.

CHAPTER
Sixteen

"What the hell is the matter with you?" Gabriel said.

Jeremy hadn't heard him step into the barn, where he was looking over Chelsea's horse, a paint. He still didn't understand why she had wanted it so badly. It was happier to just eat than be with the other horses, but the mare was one of calmest horses they owned. Nothing spooked her, and nothing excited her. The horse was also beyond slow.

Gabriel leaned against the stall door beside him. He was wearing a faded white shirt on which the lettering was starting to fade, and he turned to face Jeremy, who had been standing by the stall gate, trying to figure out what to do, because he was still freaking out over what Tiffy had said. The words were running over and over in his mind like a runaway train.

He wanted to say nothing was wrong, that hey, everything was totally fine! But he couldn't get the lie past his lips.

"Nothing, everything?" Gabriel said. "Being a father is

too much for you? Maybe you're wondering about skipping out and leaving town and how you can go about joining the other deadbeats?" He sounded so accusatory, and Jeremy just stared at his brother, seeing how he saw him, and it wasn't flattering.

"It's got nothing to do with that," he said. "Brandon is a surprise—okay, I admit it, a shock, but I'm handling it. Tiffy had nine months to get used to the idea, and I had only a second as I was getting my face bashed in by my best friend, who was intent on killing me. I mean, how fair do you think that is? She hid his very existence from me, and she did it out of spite. What we had was just sex, meaningless sex, and wham, she gets knocked up, and instead of telling me from the get-go, she gets all pissed because I'm doing what guys do. I never said I was a saint, and I made it clear from the start it was just sex. I've said that to every girl I've been with. There were never any promises of a relationship or something more or even seeing her again. I made it clear I'm not the kind of guy who's into being exclusive and dating just one girl."

He could see his dad walking their way, really digging into each step as he strode into the barn, his boots scaping on the concrete.

"And I'm sure all of this makes me sound like an asshole," he continued, "but I wasn't looking to be tied down to anyone, not now. I've got my life ahead of me, and all of this here is because she fell in love with me." He was having trouble wrapping his head around what she'd said, and at the same time, he couldn't get past the panic that had hit him at hearing it. *Like, what the fuck?* He was only nineteen, a father now, and did Tiffy have the idea that he'd be…what, walking her down the aisle? He could feel a cold sweat breaking out on his back.

"What's going on here?" His dad didn't sound happy,

but right now he didn't give a fuck, because he was still trying to get his head around what Tiffy had said, which, of course, had shut him down. He'd said nothing to her in reply, not a fucking thing, because he had suddenly freaked out. What was she really looking for? What did she really want? Love was something so far from lust that he was having trouble getting his head back to where he'd thought he'd been with Tiffy, with her despising him. Why was that so much easier to handle?

"Seems he's freaking out," Gabriel said in a way that made him sound like such an asshole.

"Yeah, you're damn right I'm freaking out," Jeremy said. "Do you have any idea what she said to me on the way out here?" He moved away from the stall and jammed his fingers in his hair, seeing the way his dad and Gabriel exchanged a glance.

"What is it, Jeremy? Because right now, this doesn't work. You don't get to do this now when you've got a kid inside the house, waiting with the mother of your child, whom I understand you dragged out here—who's done everything, from what I can see, to keep you out of her life, out of Brandon's life," his dad added. It seemed neither of them was hearing him.

"She said she was in love with me," he snapped and jabbed his chest with his hand. Both his dad and his brother stared at him as if he'd lost his mind. Maybe he had.

"I don't understand. What does that have to do with what's going on now?" Andy said, looking to Gabriel as if he could shed some light on the situation.

Jeremy couldn't answer and pulled his arms across his chest, rocking on his heels, thinking of work, school, Brandon, and then there was Tiffy. His future was supposed to be unfolding in an exciting, easy way, and now it seemed as if it was going the wrong way, with the worst-case scenario landing at his feet all at once. "I feel as if I'm being trapped," he said. "You're not hearing me. She said she didn't tell me about Brandon because she was in love with me, and I had made it so clear with everyone, every girl I had sex with, that it was just sex, it was nothing more, that I wasn't interested in anything more. Everyone said, oh, yes, totally okay, but now Tiffy says, nope, not true. She was in love with me, so now…"

"Loved you, meaning past tense," Andy added to interrupt him, tilting his head and leveling him with a pretty hard intense gaze. "Seriously, Jeremy? I hope to all hell you're more polished than this around Tiffy and your mom. With all the crap that just came out of your mouth, sometimes I swear I'm looking in a mirror and seeing myself back when I was your age. It's not a flattering picture. Looking back now, I thought I was happy with that carefree single life, when I was anything but."

This was the first time he could remember his dad ever saying something so harshly. It felt like a slap in the face.

"I never said I was a saint," Jeremy snarled.

Gabriel shook his head and went to step back as if he'd had enough. "No, you haven't," he said. "In fact, you've gone out of your way to point out to me, to everyone, what a prick you are, how you're only interested in what makes you happy, which is having the sexual gratification of fucking some woman and moving on to the next as if you're screwing your way through the population of the county."

Even his dad seemed to pause at that. Gabriel was really pissed, and it was as if Jeremy had insulted him personally. He was just being a guy, having some fun. No harm, no foul, right?

"You know what?" Andy said. "I think we all need to

just cool it right now, because this is about a little boy inside, my grandson, Brandon. What you need to get your head around, Jeremy, is that doing this, freaking out the way you are, is going to create more problems than solutions. Are you suddenly saying you don't want that boy in your life?"

Jeremy could see the way Gabriel watched him as if waiting for him to say the wrong thing. "No, it's not that. It's just that all of a sudden, I feel like when she said what she did, she had ideas about her and me…" He couldn't finish.

Andy crossed his arms over his chest and leaned in, his expression filled with impatience, needing him to finish. "You mean about having you down the aisle and marrying her?" he said, voicing his worst fear.

He couldn't swallow. He couldn't talk.

"Ah, so that's it, fear of commitment," Gabriel said, and he actually started laughing and shook his head. "Well, hate to burst your bubble, brother dear, but I guarantee you she isn't about to waste her time trying to get you anywhere near a minister. In fact, I would guess that if you did ask her to marry you, to be in any kind of committed relationship with you, she'd say no. Didn't you say her words were that she fell in love with you then, way back when she found out she was pregnant, way back when she was an idealistic fifteen-year-old?

"I've already heard enough from Dad, from everyone," Gabriel continued, "even from you, about how she was justified in not telling you because you'd already moved on to conquering other women. She was impressionable and starry eyed because the friend of her brother suddenly gave her the time of day and flashed her that cocky smile and talked her into slipping off alone from everyone, and you think for one minute that she was saying to herself, oh, yeah, this is just a one-time thing and it means nothing? I hate to tell you this, but women don't think that way, and the kind of woman who would think that way is not the kind of woman you want to be with.

"All that shallow playboy crap of yours…get over yourself! You hear me? Her falling in love with you then was back then. Pretty sure if you ask her, you'll find out you killed it by being yourself. I guess you didn't hear that part from her, because you think she's still in love with you." His brother shook his head, an odd smile on his lips. "Maybe she should say it to your face so you get it loud and clear. I can see you're not thinking clearly. She didn't tell you about Brandon, she didn't tell you she was pregnant, and she never would've told you. You never would've found out about Brandon if Alex hadn't erupted. Does that really sound like a woman who's in love with you still? Because to me, that sounds like a woman who despises you."

Gabriel lifted his hands and stepped back, shaking his head. Jeremy had never felt this divided and put in his place, but he realized what his brother had said, *past tense* and *despised*. He should've been happy. He pulled his arms tighter against his chest and took in the way his dad seemed to study Gabriel.

"Sounds to me like sides have been chosen," Jeremy said. "You're my brother. Why are you beating me up like this? I never said I was a saint, but I never lied to any girl I slept with!" He hadn't planned on yelling, and he glanced to the side and back, seeing the way his dad and brother stared at him. "I don't get you, Gabriel. I'm the one who has every right to be angry here."

Gabriel shrugged. "Do you really? From where I'm standing, I guess I don't see it that way. I remember, because I was Brandon, except I had it far harder, because when the punk who fathered me did what you've done to my mom, she had no one."

Jeremy glanced up to his dad, who was looking down at Gabriel. He wasn't sure what to make of his expression. "What?" he said and looked between them again. He'd known his mom had been a single mother when Andy married her, and then he and Chelsea had come along, but he'd never heard anything about who Gabriel's real father was, what had happened to him. He'd thought nothing of it, because he knew Andy had adopted Gabriel and they were all happy. It was kind of something they just never thought of.

His dad pulled in a breath. "It's in the past, and this isn't the same…" He turned to Jeremy. "Entirely," he added with effect. "If I could erase what happened, I would," he continued, turning to Gabriel again, "but then I wouldn't have you."

Jeremy could see how uncomfortable Gabriel was, how he wasn't on the same page about it, but then Andy jabbed a finger his way.

"And, Jeremy, your fun-filled days of bedding every woman in the county are done. You've got responsibilities now, a son, and then there's Tiffy. No one said you need to marry her. No one has even hinted at that kind of commitment, because you're only meant to come to some amicable solution that has you in Brandon's life as his father, raising him. So man up and pull yourself together, because there's one other thing I noticed with that girl." His eyes were icy blue as he took in both his sons. "She knows how to push every one of your buttons, so don't let her."

CHAPTER
Seventeen

Tiffy took the yellow mug from Laura, a beautiful woman, and breathed in the orange spicy tea as she listened to the sounds of her son's laughter and chatter coming from someplace in the house, where he was playing with Zach, Jeremy's little brother. Sarah, his little sixteen-year-old sister, was on the other side of the kitchen, pouring herself a tea, ready to join them. She was the spitting image of her mom and had the most gorgeous smile she'd ever seen. Laura had gone out of her way to make Tiffy feel welcome, and it wasn't lost on her that each of Jeremy's siblings had her eyes, the same vivid green as Brandon's.

"So glad you could come out, Tiffy, and spend some time," Laura said. "And your mom bringing Brandon out so we can get to know each other means everything. Come on, let's go sit in the living room."

Tiffy wanted to interrupt and correct her, saying that none of this had been her choice, but she found herself just nodding as she followed. Laura was a very young-looking mom, slim and curvy and gorgeous, and everything about her made Tiffy feel as if this was where she was supposed to be. She wasn't sure that was such a good thing.

She took a seat on the deep green sectional.

"This is Mom's new furniture," Sarah said, taking a seat at the other end. "Didn't you say it was time for a change?"

Laura sat in the wingback chair across from her, and all of this felt weird, awkward. She blew on the hot tea and took a polite sip, then rested the mug on a coaster on the square glass coffee table. She just nodded and took in the way mother and daughter stared at each other as if they didn't know what to say. Geez, she was really making a mess out of this.

"You know what? I should really get back. I don't think this is a great idea, come to think of it. Being here wasn't really my idea, and my mom bringing Brandon out…"

Laura lifted her hand for her to stop. "I know you didn't suggest it, but he's our grandson, and Flo and I have talked already. You should know that we want to support you any way we can. Your mom said you're looking for a job, and we've already figured out between the two of us that we can cover looking after Brandon, regardless of what you and Jeremy decide between the two of you about what you're going to do."

She just blinked, because she wasn't used to having anyone organize her life for her. She should say thank you, but the problem was that she felt she was being told what to think, and Brandon was her responsibility. She pulled in a breath when she heard footsteps and the squeak of the door, then spotted Jeremy as he walked in and seemed to hesitate as he took in his mom, his sister, and then her.

An odd expression had settled on his face when she'd said what she'd never meant to say, that she'd fallen in love with him then—way back when! Damn it, she had forgotten to stress that distinction, which was likely why that freaked-out look had evolved into something else. She didn't like the feeling she was getting.

"Uh…" He lifted his hand and then settled his megawatt shrewd gaze on her. "Tiffy, can I have a word?"

It took her a second as she sat there, considering what to say—like no! Instead, she said nothing as she stood up and took in the way Laura was glaring daggers at Jeremy. She found herself looking from mother to son. "Okay, so where? Outside or inside, but not around Brandon, or how about you just drive me and Brandon on back to town? I can pick up my mom's car where I left it at the hardware store and go home." She turned to Laura. "One of the jobs I applied for was at the hardware store because there was an ad in the paper, except I was surprised to walk in and find Jeremy running the place, and what did he do but hire me?" She turned back to Jeremy. "But no, thank you, Jeremy, because there's no way I'm working with you, for you, under you, or anywhere near you."

"Oh, for the love of God, Tiffy, I just asked to talk," he said. "Fine, you don't want a job? Done, understood. I was just trying to do the right thing and help you out." Then he swore, and she could feel how the energy in the room had ramped up again.

"Help me out?" Her fingers instinctively curled into a fist. He was uncomfortable, she could tell.

"Okay, not what I meant. That was a poor choice of words on my part. I'm just doing what I think is right. At the same time, Tiffy, you're making me feel as if anything I do or try to do is wrong," he snapped.

Laura motioned to Sarah, and they both slipped out of the room. Tiffy pulled her arms across her stomach, feeling the heated tension run through her veins. She wasn't about to back down. She wanted to yell at him, push him. She wanted him to fight back, and if she told anyone what she was thinking, what she wanted, she knew they'd say she was crazy.

"I see. Well, consider yourself off the hook. You don't need to do anything for me."

He lifted his hand. "Fine, now can we go talk, and not in here for Brandon to hear? Let's go outside for a walk," he added with an edge.

She considered saying no but just started to the door, walking right past him and pushing it open to see his dad and Gabriel in the distance, by the barn, and the horses in the field, the cattle in the distance. She had to fight the unease that came from being here.

"This way." He gestured from beside her, and though they fell into step, she made no attempt to keep up with his long strides. No, she was going to make him work for it as she pulled her arms across her chest again and slowed her walk. His hand slid over the small of her back. "Let's go out back. There's a creek out that way the horses head to. We won't be interrupted then."

She could feel him trying to hurry her, but she wasn't about to go at any pace except hers. She heard his frustration as he slowed his pace, and they came up to a gate behind the house. Jeremy opened it and motioned for her to walk through. He latched it behind him and started walking through the dirt and bits of grass that had been grazed down by the horses and cattle, she was sure. She found herself looking to see if there were animals out there, but it was just them in this field, walking. She let out a breath and felt some of the tension ease in her chest.

"The herd's been moved onto the other side of the creek, another field, to graze. The horses too, over there." He gestured to the west, and she nodded. Okay, so he understood. "You said something while we were driving in here, and we should probably talk about it. You said you fell in love with me."

So that was it. Of course, she was still kicking herself for sharing that little bit of personal trivia in such a vague way. Those had been her private thoughts from way back when, and she wished she had kept her mouth shut. It was too personal, something that had brought out her vulnerability.

"I shouldn't have said it," she said, "but you just keep pushing and pushing, so yes, I fell in love with you, Jeremy Friessen, way back when, another time in my life. Oh, yes, I agreed just to sleep with you, and I even told myself that it was just sex and I was fine with that, until I wasn't, and I realized it didn't take you long at all to pick up and move on. Another day, another girl. You know, when I heard my brother laughing about your latest conquest only days later, I realized how easy it was for you. Girls landed at your feet, in your lap, at the snap of your fingers. Of course I wasn't gonna talk to you again, and never again was I going to sleep with you, not that that would've been an option. You know the saying, fool me once… So yes, when I heard all about your exploits, I was so furious, angry with you, but mainly myself. That was then. Are you under the impression right now that I'm still in love with you? Because I can assure you I managed to get over that starry-eyed delusion."

He cocked his head toward her and then looked out into the distance. She wasn't sure what to make of his expression. She just kept telling herself these lies.

"So, Brandon. Let's talk about our son," he said.

She looked up to him, and the way he was looking down at her, he was hiding so much. She didn't have a clue what he was thinking. She nodded. "About…?"

"Come on, Tiffy. Give me a break. There's a lot we need to talk about. I want to get to know him, and him me, spend time with him." Then Jeremy stopped walking and just stared out into the distance.

"Okay, so we can work out a schedule, something like one day a week to start…"

"I want him to come and live here with me." He cut her off, and she took in the way he was watching her now, feeling as if the ground at her feet were about to give way.

She shook her head, wondering what the hell this was. "You want me to give you my son, let him move in here with you? Are you crazy? There's no way, Jeremy. You're irresponsible, an arrogant jerk…"

Then his lips were on hers, his hands on her cheeks, in her hair, pulling her closer and kissing her deeply, and good God, she'd forgotten how well he could kiss. Somehow, she managed to get her brain to kick in as she felt him sliding his hand over her ass, pulling her closer. Her hands pressed to his impressive chest, feeling the cut of his pecs, and he was stronger than she remembered. A mistake. Her traitorous hands didn't want to pull away. Somehow, in the passion and lust, feeling as if she was drowning again in that forbidden kiss she couldn't want, she turned her head and broke it, sucking in a breath, feeling all of his hardness press into her.

"Let go of me right now," she ground out. She didn't know how she found the words, but he let her go, and she almost slid to the ground, her legs weak. She took in the arrogance staring back at her, wanting to add her own reddened handprint to his face.

"I didn't mean to do that," he said and turned away as if trying to pull himself together.

She glanced around them, seeing the distance they'd walked and knowing what a bad idea this was. "Really, and what exactly did you mean to do?" she snapped, feeling the anger pulse through her. All she could do was fist her hands as her breath grew low and shallow.

This time he gave her everything as he stared down at her, his bruised jaw tight. "Dinner tonight, just you and me," he said.

She stared at him, because he was doing it again, everything unexpected, and she started to shake her head. "You want to take my son, and now you want me to go to dinner with you. Are you crazy?"

He wasn't smiling, and the way he was looking down at her, she wondered whether he remembered her naked. She had to fight the urge to pull her arms over her chest, not from fear but from want.

"You're not getting it, Tiffy," he said, going right to volatility. There seemed to be no in between with Jeremy. He was passionate, hot, and sexy, and damn it, she had to stop thinking like that. She took in the fire in his green eyes, which pinned her where she stood. Then he pulled in another breath and said, "I want you to move in, too."

CHAPTER

Eighteen

"This isn't a good idea," Tiffy said to herself. She needed to brush her hair. It was windblown and thick, and its waves could easily become unruly. She wanted to apply some blush, some shadow, maybe some mascara, and tidy up as she wiped away some of the black smudges from the mascara dotted under her eyes.

She could hear voices outside the door. She knew it was Brandon and Zach playing in the bedroom next door, and she took in the large bathroom in which she stood, with a tub and shower, in Jeremy's house, his parents' house, a place she had no intention of moving into.

"Right, so just tell him," she said, "and no more kissing —even if he can kiss. Well, that will do you no good, because that's exactly what got you into the situation you're in now." She looked in the mirror, tapping the light brown granite, seeing the want in her blue eyes and wanting to smack herself silly, because going anywhere down any road with Jeremy was a broken heart waiting to happen.

She stepped back and smoothed down her blue shirt. It was plain and ordinary, fine for job hunting, but dinner with Jeremy was the worst idea yet. Then she heard a tap on the door. "Yes?" she said, knowing she'd been a long time, and she yanked open the door to see Sarah standing there.

"Everything okay? I was walking past and thought I heard you talking, like a pep talk." Sarah was a little taller than her, and the way she looked at her, she realized there was some amusement there, she thought. Sarah reached out and touched her shoulder. "I do the same thing all the time."

Tiffy wanted to laugh as she took in the teasing smile and the light that filled Sarah's green eyes. Those eyes… She wondered if Andy and Laura knew their daughter would be wanted by every guy around. She was gorgeous, filled with kindness and empathy. So how was she related to Jeremy?

"So I heard my parents talking with Jeremy," Sarah said. "Heard you're moving in?"

She wondered whether her eyes were bugging out.

Sarah's smile widened, and she laughed. "I thought from how Jeremy said it that it sounded like his idea, not yours. So you're not moving in?" Sarah raised a brow.

Tiffy was speechless. "No," she finally said.

Sarah's smile kept widening as if she knew something Tiffy didn't. Then she reached for her arm and somehow maneuvered her down the hallway, toward voices in the kitchen. "Sorry, I can't help myself from messing with you. You see, I grew up with my brother, and I love him, but I also know that he's just like my dad. Then there's Gabriel. I've been living in a house of alphas who just take over all the time and never ask, although I'm not complaining. I do understand that look in your eyes. Word of advice, Jeremy isn't as bad as you may think. I heard enough of what happened to know he's far from a saint, but he's not a liar, he's not deceitful, and he's a good guy, so to speak, if you can get past his arrogance. So stand your ground, don't let him run you down. You need to speak up, and I've already heard you, so I know you can do it. You need to be sure he hears you and what you're saying."

Then they were standing in the opening to the kitchen, where she could see his mom seasoning a roast before putting it in the oven. Andy was lingering against the counter, and Jeremy was talking, but Gabriel saw them first. His eyes lifted to her.

"Hey, there," he said. "Well, I need to get going. Elizabeth is expecting me home. Her family is coming for dinner, which is always an experience." He stopped beside Jeremy and gave him a pointed look, then lifted his hand to his mom and dad. He rustled Sarah's hair as he walked past. "See you, kid, Tiffy," he added before he walked out the door and jogged down the steps.

"Ready?" Jeremy said to her, and she knew that his dad and mom were watching him watching her.

"Yes, but first, so we're clear, I'm not moving in. I have no intention of moving, and neither does Brandon. We're just fine where we are, at my parents' house, until I have a job and can get my own place, at which time my son and I will be moving into whatever place I can afford, just the two of us," she added with effect.

Sarah stepped away, but not before patting her shoulder as if offering her support.

"Renting a place is expensive, Tiffy," Andy said, "and we have the room here. With Chelsea now in Boston, her room is empty. If it wasn't made clear to you, that would be your own room. You can have hers, and Brandon would have Gabriel's old room. This place is big enough. Keep it in mind so you know you're not out of options."

Laura watched but didn't add anything.

Jeremy's heavy gaze lingered on her, and he said nothing.

"Understood," Tiffy replied. "Thank you for clarifying, but just the same, I can stand on my own two feet and look after my son. Also, I would've preferred to take Brandon home first to my mom and dad's, but since he's here, and I never asked if it would be…"

"He's fine here," Laura said, stepping around her husband. "In fact, he can spend the night. I can catch up with you tomorrow and bring him back to your mom's if you'd like."

Andy watched his wife protectively, she thought. She took them in and had to remind herself Jeremy wasn't his parents.

"That'll be fine," she said and nodded before dragging her gaze back to Jeremy. "So are you ready to go? Don't forget you'll need to drop me off at the hardware store so I can pick up my mom's car."

Before he could add anything, she lifted her hand to his parents and walked out the door and down the steps, seeing the dust from Gabriel's pickup in the distance. She didn't wait for Jeremy, pulling the truck door open just as his hand appeared and rested on the doorframe. She climbed in and knew he was watching her, but she put everything into doing up her seatbelt.

He was still standing there, so close she could feel his heat.

She slid her gaze up to him and did everything she could to keep her face free of any emotion. "Well, are we going or not?" she said, and the door swung shut, and she watched as he walked around the front of the truck, shaking his head. She then averted her gaze as he climbed in the driver's side and closed the door. She focused everything on breathing in and out.

He started the truck and spun it around, giving it gas, heading down the dirt driveway. He took the bumps and ruts in the dirt road a little fast, and she bounced a bit on the seat.

"About earlier, I didn't mean to grab you and kiss you like that," he said, which was exactly what she didn't want to hear.

"So what exactly did you mean to do, if I might be so bold as to ask?"

That brought an odd smile to his lips. She wasn't sure if he was laughing at her or ready to wring her neck. The latter, she thought, from the way he squeezed the wheel.

"Okay, fine, I don't know what it is about you, but being around you twists me into knots and makes me lose my mind. I can't be reasonable around you. You know how to get under my skin, Tiffy, and since we're talking about this, you're the only girl I've slept with that I can remember every single detail about. So tell me, Tiffy, why do you insist on pushing my buttons? Because you do, and you're so frickin' smart that you know just what to say."

She found herself staring at him. This wasn't what she'd expected. "Why are we still talking about this, Jeremy? I thought we were supposed to be discussing Brandon, but suddenly you want to take me for dinner, you're grabbing me and kissing me, and don't think I didn't see how you were freaking out when I said I had fallen in love with you, as if you thought I meant now. You were spooked and running, and that was enough for me. So what if I said to you that I have feelings for you, Jeremy? What if I said, yeah, the thought of sleeping with you again excites me, and at the same time it makes me want to weep, because I would be the one alone again after? You're not the kind of guy who settles. You made it clear, and I can see how you wish you were anywhere but here."

He was leaning against the door as he drove, one hand on the wheel, and he shook his head but had yet to say anything.

May as well go for the kill and put an end to all this dancing around, she thought, so she said, "And what would you do if I said, okay, yeah, I'll move in, be there with you, and we'll raise Brandon together, but I have some ground rules first: You say goodbye to every other woman out there, no dating, no sleeping around? You become exclusive to me and Brandon and do everything to build something even if it is just being a father." Pushing and setting down these hard rules she knew he'd never agree to was exhilarating. In fact, he'd just say no and tell her to get lost, because there was no way this would happen. Dancing around her feelings was killing her. Best to push and drive him away for good. "In fact, you know what? Forget moving into your parents' place and sleeping in your sister's room, where you're down the hall and I'm like an uninvited guest with Brandon. You and me get a place together, and you have to tell everyone that I'm the mother of your child, that Brandon is your son, and let everyone know we're your priority. In fact, I want a ring on my finger…"

"What…?"

The way he said it, it took everything she had to keep the smile from tugging at her lips. She should stop, but it was too much fun. She expected him to just drive her to her car and leave. Forget dinner, and then she would go home and get back to her list and plans and forget all of this nonsense about trying to create something amicable with Jeremy. He'd be out of her life.

"Yup, a ring…" She held up her left hand and wiggled her finger, knowing she was going too far. "And commitment to me, and a holiday wedding. Like, why wait? It'll be legit then, and—"

"You got it, baby!" he snapped.

It took her a second as she stared at him. He pulled his gaze from the road to her and back, and her brain still hadn't quite figured it out. He couldn't have said what he did. "But…" she started.

"Hey, you just laid it all out, what you want, what you need, and I just said you got it, all of it."

"No!" she bit out, her mouth open, because he'd completely turned the tables on her.

"What do you mean, no? I just agreed to every one of your terms, and just to be clear, I have a few of my own."

This was crazy. She just stared at the arrogance that had completely yanked the rug right out from under her. He wasn't serious. He couldn't be serious.

"You too. It goes both ways, Tiffy. You're mine one hundred percent, all of you, which means we get a place, move in, become parents together, and you're in my bed. If you think I'm going to become a monk, you're sadly mistaken, and if you were under some impression that we'd coexist as roommates while the rest of the world sees us together, married, you may as well get that idea out of your head. So you'll share my bed and be a willing participant. You want all that, guess what? Sex comes with it, anytime and anywhere I want it."

She had to remind herself to close her mouth, which was gaping from the shock as she took in the heat in his gaze, the way his green eyes filled with passion and fire and stubborn strength. She'd pushed him too far now, knowing her mistake, and the tension, the sexual tension she'd refused to feel, just ratcheted up to a hundred. The way he watched her, it was as if he already had her, had already bedded her again, already had her body wanting it so badly, so much that she had to force herself to look forward as she brought her hand over her stomach, feeling the heat of the blush that she knew she couldn't hide.

"And you know what, Tiffy? You may have been bluffing, trying to push me the other way and out of your life, but I'd say it just backfired on you. Even your reaction, your body, everything…you can't hide how much you want it. Nope, Tiffy, I agree to all your conditions with my added additional terms. Ball's in your court, baby. So what'll it be?"

CHAPTER
Nineteen

What had he been thinking? Or not thinking, considering he seemed to be digging himself into one hole after another with Tiffy. Instead of taking her for dinner, he'd ordered takeout at the Burger Bar and driven them out to the lake, the same spot where all of this had started: a high school party, a bonfire, some beer, and two stupid teens getting their kicks by the water. Now, three years later, sitting on the tailgate of his pickup about two hundred yards from the said secluded spot, he couldn't take his eyes from Tiffy, who took careful bite after bite of the house burger and had yet to utter one word.

Including no.

He couldn't get the thought from his mind of what it would be like to have Tiffy under him again, inside her, letting her satisfy all his needs. He cleared his throat and jumped down from the tailgate, feeling the discomfort. He needed to pull it together or he was going to be doing something he shouldn't want. He tossed the balled-up wrapper from his burger into the bag and realized that

Tiffy was deliberately doing everything to keep her gaze averted.

"I was serious," he said and pulled in a breath, waiting for the freak-out to start again, but this time, when she finally swung her gaze back to him, he wasn't sure what he was seeing.

She narrowed her eyes. Freaking out, angry, despising the ground he walked on?

"I guess I want to know if you were, too, or was that you playing me?"

She opened her mouth and then shut it, wrapped up the rest of her burger, and tucked it back in the bag. He stood right in front of her, so close he could feel her heat, and she still hadn't answered.

"I could take that two ways," he said. "You were playing your own little game, or deep down, it's what you want. So let's go with the latter. A ring, you said. Everyone will know you're mine, that Brandon's mine, that we're together, living together, sleeping together."

Her gaze flicked up, and he could see the flicker of heat. She couldn't hide her wanting. Maybe she did still love him, after all. There was a fine line between love and hate.

"You're moving too fast," she said. "We're supposed to be talking about Brandon." She went to slip down, but he moved in closer, his hands on her knees, and he could feel the tremble.

"We did talk about Brandon, and then you took it to another level of commitment. So that's what we're talking about now, or is it you're trying to backpedal because you're the one who's terrified of something happening here?"

She gazed up at him, and he wondered when her smart

mouth was going to kick in. "I'm not the one who's terrified," she said. "I'd say you are."

He slid his hands over her knees and thighs and pulled her forward so he could step between her legs, which now dangled over the edge. He slid his hand around her back, and she was so close to him that he could feel her warm breath, feel the reaction to him that she couldn't hide. At the same time, she lowered her gaze, taking in his lips, his chest, his shoulders, looking anywhere but at his face.

He lifted his other hand and touched the side of her head, brushing back her hair and just watching her, waiting for what she'd do next. He skimmed her ear and ran the back of his fingers down over her cheek, her jawline, until she finally lifted her gaze up to him, and he didn't expect the shyness and uncertainty he saw there now. Instead of stepping back and letting her have a minute, he lowered his head and waited for just a second for her to say no, stop.

She didn't, so he pressed his lips to hers and tasted her, kissing her deeply and really sinking into her. One hand settled on his shoulder, her other in his hair, as he slid his hands around her back again and pulled her right to the edge, right to him, so she could feel every hard inch of him. He couldn't remember ever wanting anyone more.

He touched her everywhere, running his hands over her breasts, hearing her soft sighs as he broke the kiss and ran his mouth, his lips, his tongue down the side of her neck. He pulled at her shirt, grabbing the edges and lifting it over her head. She pulled off her bra and he his shirt before tasting and touching the perfection of her breasts, and her hands went around his head. He could hear her, feel the way she leaned back and let him have her and take what he wanted. And he wanted her.

He didn't know who pulled what off. He yanked off

her shoes and pulled off her jeans, vaguely hearing them hit the ground. She had his zipper down, and his jeans slid down his ass. She held all his hardness in her hand. He wanted her, he was ready, and he wasn't going to wait.

"Damn it, condom." He swore under his breath, reaching his wallet in his back pocket and pulling it out, but she took it from him, tore open the wrapper, and covered him. Then she leaned back on the truck bed as he pulled her closer, slid inside her, and moved. Her eyes were on his, her hands on his shoulders, her arms over his head as he rode her and took her over and over, doing what he did well, fucking a woman, except this time as he held her, he leaned down and kissed her tenderly, slowly. He felt her around him and wondered if, just maybe, there was something more.

CHAPTER
Twenty

It was late when he pulled in at home and stepped out of his truck.

The house was dark, and everyone would be asleep. He could hear the horses in the corral close to the house, the cattle in the distance, and the sounds of the night. There were crickets, too, something he didn't hear often as he climbed the steps, the wood creaking under him. He pulled open the screen door and the inside door, which had been left unlocked for him, then stepped into the darkened house.

Jeremy had just closed the door and slid the deadbolt when a light came on. It was his mom walking down the hall in her green flowered housecoat, barefoot. She said nothing as she crossed her arms and stopped just a foot away.

"Brandon is asleep in Chelsea's room," she finally said.

He just nodded.

"And Tiffy?" she asked. The way she was watching him, he wondered if she was disappointed. It bothered him more than he'd realized. There was so much about his mom, about what had happened before he was born, that he didn't understand.

"Dropped her off," he said. "She's on her way home."

Laura nodded, her lips firmed. He expected to see his dad come out next, but there was no one.

"Mom, can I ask you something?"

The way her green eyes flashed with interest and seemed to relax, he wondered how she'd react. "Of course, what is it?"

"It's just something Gabriel mentioned, and then Dad, I guess. This whole scenario with Tiffy has you seeing me in an unflattering light. I know you're angry with me, and I'm not sure how to get you to understand that it wasn't about you and what happened. If I'd have known…"

His mom stepped toward him and seemed to relax a bit. "I know that, Jeremy. I know you wouldn't have turned your back on her if you'd known. Your dad did explain that to me, and it wasn't about you stepping up on your own, which we hoped you would have. It was that if we'd known, Tiffy wouldn't have been off in another place. It's not the same as what I went through, but at the same time, it is, because she was still a mother at sixteen. The only difference is that Tiffy still had her family. She had the support network I never had."

He just stared at his mom. She'd never spoken of her family even though he'd often wondered what had happened to them. "Your parents…" he started.

His mom stepped closer and rested her hand on his arm to stop him. "Are not Flo and Wayne," she said. "So what are your plans with Tiffy? I mean, you left here with her, and the last I heard was you trying to tell her she was moving in here."

Laura gestured to the living room, and he took that as his cue to follow her. He did, because making right with his mom was high on his list of priorities, up there with making it work with Tiffy, even though he didn't really understand what it was he'd done to make her so angry at him.

"Well, it may have gone a little further than that," he said. "One of the things Tiffy does is she knows how to push my buttons and get under my skin. Dad pointed that out, because she listed off a bunch of demands that I knew she thought would have me running the other way." He still couldn't believe he wasn't. He couldn't believe he was still having this conversation with his mom and not freaking out, the kind of commitment he didn't think he could do.

"Oh, and am I going to like this?" his mom said, and he took in her frown from where she sat on the sectional, her feet curled up to the side.

Jeremy took the other end, facing her. "Her terms were that she and Brandon come first, and everyone knows she's the one and only, except I may have turned the tables on her and laid out a few terms of my own." He could see from the way his mom was watching him that she may have the wrong idea. "Relax, Mom. I think you'd be happy."

She glanced away, pulling in a breath. "I don't think you get it, Jeremy. It's not necessarily about me, and you shouldn't be making whatever decision it is that you're making unless it's what you want and is in the best interest of that little boy. So if what you decided is to make me happy…"

"Marriage, Mom." He cut her off, and she stared at him as if she hadn't heard him. "And it's not for you or Dad. It's for me, Tiffy, and Brandon. She's under my skin, and it's not only the right thing…"

"Wait, Jeremy. Marriage is a huge step, not something

you should be running into. Raising Brandon together and being responsible are all that's needed. Don't you think that's a little over the top? Your dad and I got married because of a situation that he felt responsible for, and I'm not saying this so you misunderstand, because I love your father, he's the love of my life, and I know he loves me so deeply now, but it wasn't always that way. In fact, before I had you and your sister, we weren't together. I had left because I felt like an obligation. For a woman to feel like that and be treated like that is definitely not the reason to get married. All I can say is if you're doing this out of some misguided sense of obligation, please don't, because it will backfire on you. Instead of doing the right thing, you could turn the entire relationship between you and Tiffy and Brandon into one of resentment, and that's not what Brandon needs."

Okay, not what he'd expected. He just stared at his mom and then stood up, and he thought he caught Tiffy's scent. It was in his head and around him, and he wondered if his dad had felt any of what he was feeling when he'd first met his mom. "I hear what you're saying, Mom, and I wouldn't have agreed to anything if it wasn't what I wanted. You know what? I think I'm going to turn in."

His mom said nothing else at first, but she stood up as well, walked around the square table, and then stopped beside him, resting her hand on his forearm. "Good, but then, this is your choice, as long as it's the right one and only yours to make. Let me know if I can do anything to help." She patted his arm and took a step back.

"Actually, Mom, there is something," he said.

She turned to face him, her beautiful green eyes free of the earlier hurt and anger. "Okay."

"It's about a ring."

Her expression was questioning, and he shrugged.

"For Tiffy," he clarified.

His mom offered him a slow smile. "You know what? I might just be able to help you with that. Oh, and before I forget, your sister called tonight. She wants you to call her. Goodnight, Jeremy."

Then his mom walked softly down the hall to her bedroom, and he listened to the door close.

He flicked off the light and strode down the darkened hallway and into his bedroom, and he was just closing the door when his cell phone buzzed. He pulled it from his pocket and stared at the screen, seeing Chelsea's ID.

"Hey, sis, thanks for calling."

"So sorry I took so long," she said. "I wasn't ignoring you, just been out of cell range at a condo in the Rockies Ric dragged me off to. So what's up? Talking with Dad tonight, he mentioned something about a kid, yours?"

Out of all his family, Chelsea had always been there for him, whether they fought, disagreed, or anything. It didn't matter. She understood him and he her in a way no one else in the family did.

"Yeah, it's kind of a long story, and let's just say one I just found out about. He's two, he looks just like me—and I'm getting married," he said, hearing the laughter on the other end.

He sat on his bed and started to tell his sister everything.

CHAPTER
Twenty~One

Tiffy was freaking out. Her palms were sweaty even though it was far from cool, and she'd slept in fits, in what she thought were chunks of time here and there as she tossed and turned on the hard futon. It was rock hard and uncomfortable, and she didn't have a little boy kicking her. She could still feel Jeremy Friessen inside her and was horrified at how she'd let him screw her again at that same lake—not just once, because then she could've chalked that up to a simple slip, a sudden moment where she'd lost her mind and could say, *What the hell were you thinking?*

No, she'd helped him strip out of the rest of his clothes to join her completely naked outside on a blanket he'd had tucked under his seat on the ground, where anyone could have found them if they'd decided to drive out to the middle of nowhere for their own evening romp. She'd let him roll onto his back, where he let her take the lead, sinking down on top of him and riding him as if this was what they did. To make it worse, she couldn't deny how much she'd craved his touch, his kiss, and the sex they'd had again.

Did they talk?

Not one word. Evidently, what they were better at was having sex. He'd fallen asleep, and she'd let him, listening to the sound of his heart as he pulled each breath in and out, her head on his chest for an hour before she'd gotten dressed and stared at his naked perfection in the dusky light before waking him and telling him to drive her back to her mom's car so she could go home.

She slapped her hand over her face, her eyes, thinking back with horror as the sun streamed through the blinds. "What were you thinking? Now what? Just look at the trouble you've gotten yourself into. Your mouth, Tiffy, has gotten you into some doozies before, and you thought you could send him running for the hills? Wow, he sure turned the tables on you." She gestured to the stucco ceiling, hearing footsteps creak in the hallway and knowing someone was up. She hoped they weren't listening to her talk to herself. Then there was Brandon. She needed to get him.

She sat up, feeling the ache in her back, and tossed back the covers before sliding out to the floor, her bare feet on the carpet. She rummaged her bag for clean underwear, a bra, a T-shirt, and took in her clothes, which she'd tossed in a heap last night. She finally just reached for her clean black jeans.

Peeking out into the hall, she saw the open bathroom door and stepped out. The floor squeaked, and she sprinted into the bathroom and shut the door behind her, flicking the lock and leaning against it. She let out a breath and banged her head against the door. "Stupid, stupid Tiffy! What were you thinking?" she said under her breath before pushing away, setting her clean clothes on the vanity, and turning on the shower.

She waited for the hot water to kick in before stepping under the spray, allowing the hot water to run over her sore muscles, which were wound so tight from the worry, from the lack of sleep, from stepping into Jeremy Friessen's web.

"Argh!" She pressed her hands to her face, because she couldn't get his face, his touch, everything of him, from her mind. Worse, she knew there was nothing about what had happened that would lead to a fairytale ending, because Jeremy Friessen was not the prince who showed up with a glass slipper. He was the guy who would forever have one foot out the door.

She reached for the shampoo and scrubbed her scalp a little harder than usual, then used conditioner and ran a bar of soap over herself before lathering up and rinsing off just as she felt the water turn from hot to warm. She turned off the shower and took her time drying off and pulling on her clothes. She ran her hand over the steamed-up mirror as she brushed her teeth and froze when she spotted the red mark on her neck.

"You jerk…" She let the words fall away as she took in the hickey, the size of a grape—no, a small orange, with a shape that resembled Texas. She slapped her hand over it as she spit in the sink. There it was, no hiding it. She rinsed her mouth and ran through her mind what other shirts she'd packed, as there was nothing that could hide what he'd done. Everyone would know what she had participated in, and everyone knew that she'd been out with Jeremy. She rinsed off her toothbrush and tossed it in the cup, then dried her hands, ran a brush through her wet hair, and tousled it a bit before arranging the damp ends to hide her neck.

"There, that will work. Just keep your head down and

don't toss your hair around, and no one will see." Then she pulled open the door, bent down to pick up her nightshirt and shorts, and carried them into her bedroom.

She pulled at the ends of her hair again before stepping back into the hall, hearing voices in the kitchen—her mom, her dad, and Alex. She could smell the coffee, and she walked right for the coffeepot and kept her back to everyone as she lifted a mug from the shelf and poured herself a cup.

"Didn't hear you come in last night," Flo said. "Did you have fun? I talked to Laura last night, and she said you went out for dinner with Jeremy. Also heard he asked you to move in."

She turned around and leaned against the counter, holding her mug, taking a sip, seeing the way her brother stared at her, and her dad too, with an odd look on his face. Her mom was also staring at her as if she was losing her grip on reality.

She shrugged. "He did, but I was clear that I …" She stopped talking because Alex actually tilted his head, looking at her.

He narrowed his eyes and lifted his finger. "What is that?" he snapped, and she realized what he'd seen. "Is that a hickey?"

This time she took in the way her dad raised his brows and glanced to her mom, who only shook her head as she took another swallow of coffee.

"Okay, and if it is?" she replied, exactly what she shouldn't have said.

Her brother made a rude noise and shook his head.

"So I take it you and Jeremy came to an understanding, among other things," her mom said, glancing to Alex, who reached for his keys and was picking up his bagel when she heard a knock at the front door. Wayne slid off the stool and went to answer it.

Understanding wasn't the word. "Well…" she started.

"Mommy!" Brandon raced in and over to her. "I had so much fun, and Gramps took me out to show me a pony!"

She put down her coffee and lifted him, and he wrapped his legs around her. She spotted Jeremy walk in, her dad behind him. His eyes went right to her, and from that one glance, she felt his brand on her. She held her son tighter, but he squirmed to get down, and she let him, dropping her gaze, but not before she saw Alex look between her and Jeremy as if he still needed some explanation as to what was going on. He leaned back on the island, no longer about to leave. Instead, he took a bite of his bagel and waited. For what, she didn't know.

"You let him ride a pony?" she said, squeezing her fists and feeling as if she wasn't being heard, but Jeremy shook his head.

"No, Dad wouldn't do that. He knew you were upset about the horse thing. I told him we'd ease you in, get you comfortable around them so you see there's nothing to worry about. He just showed him, is all."

She opened her mouth to say no, and why did it sound as if he had plans that concerned her? She took in Brandon climbing on the stool beside his dad, but her mom lifted him down.

"Go on and play with your toys and let the adults talk," Flo said before kissing Brandon's head. She put him down, and he made a roaring sound as he hopped out of the kitchen. She didn't miss how Jeremy's gaze tracked Brandon's movements.

"So did Tiffy share the news?" Jeremy said. He was looking at her again, and she reached for her mug and squeezed it, feeling the heat before dropping her gaze a second time. She felt everyone's eyes on her again.

"No, what news? What's going on?" Flo asked. "Tiffy?"

"Anything to do with the hickey on her neck?" Alex said. She hoped he wasn't about to come out swinging again. "Seems to have your stamp all over it."

"Uh, sorry," Jeremy said. "Kind of lost my head, but yeah, it does." He slid his gaze to her, and she held her mug with one hand as she slid the other over the lip of the counter, pulling in a breath to say…what? It was nothing, but it was everything.

"Tiffy and I are moving in together, and…" He reached in his pocket and pulled out a small box, then flicked it open, and she spotted a ring.

What?

"And we're getting married," he finished.

Huh?

She wondered if the shock on her brother's face could in any way match hers. Jeremy walked around the island, holding the box, and she was stuck on how he'd managed to pick up a ring between the previous night and now. She had thought all of that sparring last night had been just that and would amount to nothing, putting them back to square one.

Then he pulled the ring from the box, took the mug in her hands, and rested it on the counter before he lifted her left hand, and she just stared at it, at her hand and then up to Jeremy. "You said a ring, a place together, and we already fulfilled my demands last night, everything I want," he said.

She had to breathe from the way he was looking at her, as if he could take her to bed again.

"Are you going to keep your end?" he said. "Because I meant every word, and last night kind of proved that we work." He was holding the ring over her finger, and she couldn't get her tongue to move, so she nodded. He slid the ring on, though it was a little on the big side.

"How, when…?" was all she could get out.

"It was my mom's, the first ring my dad ever gave to her. Until I can afford something more…" he started, and she wasn't sure what she saw there, so she nodded.

"You really mean all of this, just us?" she said. "Really, you're marrying me and not looking to have one foot out the door? Because I won't do that, I won't have Brandon see something that is…"

"Fake."

She nodded.

He lifted his hand to her chin and slid it through her damp hair, a slight smile on his lips as he took in the mark he'd left on her. "Oh, I think last night showed both of us that there's nothing fake about this."

"So no freaking out," she added, hearing Alex curse behind them.

He glanced to Alex and then gave everything back to her. "No, but until we find a place, you, me, and Brandon are moving to the ranch," he said, then lowered his head to kiss her. He stopped a breath away and glanced back to her brother. "You good with this?"

She noted that her mom and dad had slipped out of the room. Alex slid his gaze over to her and back to Jeremy, then lifted his keys again and jabbed his finger toward him.

"You make her happy, and I mean damn fucking happy, because if you don't, the next time I come gunning for you, I won't miss." Then he slowly allowed a smile to touch his face. His gaze slipped over to her. "Tiffy, you want this?"

What could she say—no, wait, this is too fast? She pulled in a breath. "Yes."

Alex strode out of the room and said goodbye to his parents and Brandon, and that left just her and Jeremy, who was watching her so intently.

"Just so we're clear, I'm not working for you, and I need to find a job," she said.

"Fine," he replied, then dropped his gaze to her lips and leaned down and kissed her. When he pulled back, she looped her arms around his neck, feeling his discomfort pressing into her, but she realized he wasn't running.

"So you really mean all this?" she said.

"Yeah, Tiffy. Go pack your things, because when I said we're living together, I meant right now, you, me, and Brandon. Then we'll figure everything else out as we go."

He leaned in again and pressed a kiss to her lips, pulling her away from the counter, his hands on her hips as she went on her tiptoes and kissed him again.

"You know, living at the ranch with your parents isn't ideal," she said. She wasn't sure what to make of the wicked smile that touched his lips.

"Nope, but at least you'll be in my bed with me, and my room is at the other end of the house," he added, and she settled against him again, went on her tiptoes, and this time she kissed him, letting his hand slide over her ass, letting him hold her in a way she'd never expected would ever happen with Jeremy.

CHAPTER
Twenty~Two

" I 'm back!"

Jeremy took in Dorothy as she strode through the front door of the hardware store, pulling off sunglasses and sporting an incredible tan.

"So tell me all the news. What did I miss?" she said.

Cady glanced his way, as did Ruth, who was holding a box of metal hinges.

"Well, Jeremy is getting married," Ruth said, while Cady frowned, "and he has a son, a two-year-old son."

Dorothy glanced from him, to Ruth, to Cady. She stepped over closer, allowing her gaze to run from his head to his toes. "Wow, you move fast there, Friessen. When I said find yourself a girl, I didn't mean shack up and have a kid. I was only gone two weeks."

He noticed then that Cady and Ruth had slipped away, and he thought about how he'd never expected to feel what he was feeling. "It's a long story," he said, and he took in the way Dorothy seemed to be thinking as she slid her gaze back to him.

"I just bet it is. So does she make you happy?" She

pressed her big sunglasses to the top of her floppy hat, and he thought of waking up with Tiffy pressed against him, the sex that he'd never expected to be so good. He thought of the first time he'd gotten her on Chelsea's horse and the way she'd trusted him to not let her fall. Then there was Brandon, his son, a handful, and he loved him more than life itself.

"More than I expected," he said. "More than I thought was possible."

"So marriage, really?" she said, making it sound as if it was something he hadn't seriously considered.

"Yeah, marriage. When it's right, it's right."

"Wow, a kid, marriage, and love." Dorothy shook her head, and he wondered if she knew how right she'd been about the order in which it had happened.

"Yup, exactly as you said."

"Oh, the women will weep!" she teased as she walked away.

Maybe they would, but Jeremy had all he needed, and for the first time in his life, he understood what his dad had meant. He'd thought he was happy before, but he hadn't understood what true happiness was until now.

Ground Rules

With their wedding less than a week away, Jeremy and Tiffy discover they're not on the same page when it comes to raising their son and dealing with the challenges that come their way. In true Friessen fashion, when Jeremy tries to establish ground rules, he soon learns that Tiffy isn't the kind of woman anyone can tell what to do, and his strong personality could have her calling off the wedding and walking the other way.

Chapter 1

"This is like an overcrowded boarding house. Instead of downsizing with kids moving out, we seem to be going the wrong way," Andy Friessen said to his wife, Laura, who was setting out a mixed bowl of fruit on the kitchen counter. It was exactly 7:45 a.m., when everyone arrived at once for breakfast.

There was bread on the counter, and Jeremy had dibs on the toaster. Brandon was jumping up and down beside him, wearing a pull-up, his nose running. He yanked on Jeremy's T-shirt, hanging off him, wanting sugary Nutella on his toast. Jeremy had let him try it the week before, and now every day was a fight to get him to eat anything else for breakfast, lunch, dinner, or even snacks.

"No, Brandon, you can have some cereal instead," Tiffy said as she stepped into the kitchen, freshly showered, her dark hair wet and combed back. She was dressed in blue jeans and a yellow cotton shirt, whereas Jeremy was looking rough, his hair a mess, and he seemed to have pulled on yesterday's clothes. He said nothing, simply tossed Tiffy a sharp glance over his shoulder as he rested his hands on the counter.

Andy wasn't sure what he was seeing in that exchange between them: tiredness, tension, trouble.

Tiffy grabbed some bowls from the cupboard and filled them with cornflakes from the pantry, then pulled the milk from the fridge.

"No, I want Nutella!" Brandon howled.

Andy took a swallow of coffee and wondered how much sleep Brandon had gotten, as he seemed on the verge of a meltdown from the way he was whining. How much longer would it be until Jeremy gave in no matter what Tiffy said? Jeremy was still facing the toaster and said nothing.

"Dad, remember I have to stay late after school. You said you'd pick me up?" Sarah hurried into the kitchen, her blond hair styled and pinned up, and he noticed she was wearing more makeup than usual. Her blue and white blouse was unbuttoned to reveal a tank underneath, showing more cleavage than he thought was necessary for his sixteen-year-old daughter.

"And why can't you take the bus like your brother and everyone else?" Andy said.

"Remember it's the last day before Christmas, and I'm part of the club that's making sure all the Christmas boxes are ready. The volunteers will be picking them up before dinner."

"So is that why you're dressed the way you're dressed, for Christmas boxes?" Andy lifted his cup to take another swallow, not pulling his gaze from Sarah. She was too attractive for her own good. Maybe that was why he was fighting the urge to lock her up until she was thirty.

"It's about Reese," Laura said to him in a low voice,

sliding her hand over his lower back as she stepped around him, wearing a pink sweater and blue jeans.

Zach hurried in, reaching around Sarah and shoving his hand into the bread to pull out two slices. He moved behind Jeremy, who was now trying to butter the bread despite Brandon holding his leg and swinging back and forth. There was honey, peanut butter, and...yup, the Nutella was now out on the counter. Which one would he pick?

"Reese? Who is Reese?" Andy said, taking in Sarah as she peeled an orange. Then he darted a gaze over to his wife, who was pouring her own coffee. A teasing smile touched the edges of her lips. He wasn't ready for another of his daughters to start dating. He was still trying to come to terms with the fact that Chelsea was now with a man he never would've chosen for her in a million years. He thought back to the loser boyfriend Chelsea had dated at sixteen, Boone Hudson, whom he still wanted to see six feet under.

"Seriously, Jeremy, the bus is coming! Move out of the way," Zach said as he reached around and shoved his bread in the toaster.

Jeremy sighed and tossed a dark look his brother's way as he opened the jar of Nutella, and Andy found himself shaking his head. The words *Don't do it* were on the tip of his tongue.

"He's no one, Dad," Sarah said. "Okay, I've got to go." She shoved a piece of orange in her mouth and started out of the kitchen.

Tiffy reached for Brandon and lifted him, which didn't go over well, as he let out a howl and kicked his legs, going right to a DEFCON 1 meltdown. Andy wanted to plug his ears as he winced.

"Jeremy, stop giving in to him," Tiffy snapped. "He's

sick. He's not having any more of that crap. This is ridiculous! He won't eat anything else now because of that. This isn't helping."

Zach somehow had managed to slip in and grab his toast from the toaster and was hurrying out and around the corner, running out the door for the bus. Andy was able to spot him through the window, backpack looped over his shoulder, his coat under his arm, eating two pieces of toast as he ran past his sister to the end of the driveway at the road, where the bus picked them up.

"Brandon, I told you already your choice is cereal, nothing else," Tiffy added as Brandon tried to push out of her arms.

Brandon let out another howl as Tiffy held him, kicking and flailing. Andy saw it coming a second too late, as Brandon reached around Tiffy and smacked the bowls on the island, sending them flying and shattering on the floor.

"Tiffy, don't move!" Laura said sharply. "You're barefoot. One step and you'll cut yourself. Let me grab the broom." She flicked her gaze to Andy, and he knew she wanted him to do something.

Jeremy was still holding out the toast to Brandon, smeared with enough Nutella that it would put anyone into a sugar coma. A warning was on the tip of Andy's tongue again: *Seriously, don't do it.*

"Jeremy, no," Tiffy snapped. She was getting ready to fight, the tension only adding to Brandon's temper tantrum. He somehow grabbed the toast and licked the spread, and Andy could see the sparks flicker to a slow ignition between Jeremy and Tiffy.

"Okay, you, that's about enough," Andy said as he set his coffee down and stepped around the island to reach for Brandon, taking him from Tiffy. At the same time, he took the toast and tossed it into the sink, which of course had Brandon howling again. "Seriously, Brandon, give my ears a break," Andy said. "And, Jeremy, you need to listen to Tiffy. Parenting doesn't work when you're battling each other. Brandon isn't going to listen if you keep giving in to him, because he knows that he just has to put up a fuss and become a monster and you'll give him whatever he wants. That spread you've been feeding him for a week is nothing but pure sugar. Why do we even have it in the house?"

He turned to Laura, who was sweeping up the shards from the shattered bowls after dumping the big pieces in the garbage. Tiffy stood still and barefoot with the oddest expression on her face. Jeremy did too, and he realized how tired his son looked. How much sleep were they getting?

"Zach grabbed it at the store, remember?" Laura said.

Jeremy lifted the jar and took in the label as Brandon whimpered and cried.

"If you read the label, you'll likely see the first ingredient is sugar," Andy said. "There's nothing in there that Brandon should be eating. He's sick, and now you're going to have to stick to your guns and back Tiffy up, and…" He caught a whiff of something and realized Brandon needed to be changed. "Take your son and change him, clean him up, and put him back to bed."

He held Brandon out to Jeremy, taking in his grandson's teary eyes. Jeremy made a face at the odor and looked not too keen as he took Brandon, holding him out, and stepped out of the kitchen. All Andy could hear was Brandon crying and arguing incoherently, the bathroom door closing, and then water running.

"Well, thanks for that," Tiffy said, unamused, just as Laura finished clearing up the floor and emptied the dustpan of broken bits into the garbage.

"You're both looking tired," Andy said. Laura tossed a meaningful glance his way.

Tiffy was twisting the ring on her finger and glancing off to the side.

"You need to stand your ground with Jeremy," Laura added, though Andy could tell by her tone that she wasn't impressed. "This is new to him…"

"You mean the parent thing," Tiffy replied, cutting Laura off, not trying to hide her frustration. Okay, so she and Jeremy were having some struggles. She firmed her lips and shook her head. "Sorry, that came out kind of rude. I'm just tired. You're right." She rested her hand on the island and rolled her shoulders, which did little to shake off the tension even he could see she was carrying.

"Keep in mind, Tiffy, you've been doing this a while," Andy said. "Jeremy will catch on." He hoped so, or else he'd be pulling him aside and sitting him down, because even he could see that Jeremy gave in whenever Brandon wanted something. Actually, come to think of it, he'd sit him down anyway and have a father–son chat about what it meant to be a father.

"Will he? Because as I see it, he's about becoming the good guy, giving Brandon anything and everything he wants. It's not a popularity contest, but I'm wondering if that's what he's trying to do. He doesn't listen to what I say to Brandon, and it doesn't matter what it is. If I say no, he says yes."

Andy found himself taking in Laura, whose mouth gaped for a second. Tiffy shook her head. It seemed the honeymoon was over before it had even begun.

"Sorry, that was…" She shrugged again, and he just stared and waited. "He's your son, and…and I really need to go and get ready. I have work, and…" She gestured and then stepped awkwardly out of the kitchen.

He listened to her footsteps and took in his wife, who was staring at the empty doorway.

"Well, that's not good," Laura said. "Maybe you should sit your son down and have a talk with him, because as I see it, this is going in the wrong direction. He needs to start listening and working with Tiffy. You know they're not even married yet, and in case you haven't noticed, it's been a while since either of them mentioned the wedding—you know, the one that's supposed to be happening sometime next week if the two of them would figure it out and decide?" Laura ran her hand over his arm, and he took in the amazing green eyes of the woman who was the love of his life, the mother of his children. Never in a million years could he have pictured himself with her when he was Jeremy's age, because at nineteen, he'd been an arrogant jerk who played the field. Yeah, he really hadn't been much different than his son was now.

"Was hoping I wouldn't have to," Andy said. "He's got to make his own mistakes, figure things out himself, kind of like I did."

Laura winced, and a soft smile touched her lips. How had he ever gotten so lucky?

"Maybe so, but as I see it, this should be an exciting time. We should be tiptoeing around them because they can't keep their hands off each other, but instead I've noticed the distance between them is only growing wider. So talk to your son, find out what's going on, and if he doesn't want this, to get married…"

He waited for what his wife would say, pulling in another breath as she stepped in closer. He settled his coffee on the island so he could wrap his arms around her. "Then they shouldn't be getting married," he finished for her.

She nodded, her chin resting on his chest as she looked

up at him. "Yeah, they shouldn't, but they do need to come to an understanding and settle on some clear boundaries with Brandon. If they don't, none of this is going to work, and every day could be a repeat of this morning."

Laura slid her arms over his shoulders and rose up on her tiptoes. It was automatic to lean down and kiss her. Then she stepped away. "Oh, and don't forget Sarah after school—and don't embarrass her! That boy Reese will be there with her, and she likes him. Just so you know, our daughter has asked me to talk to you and tell you that you scare Reese and every boy who's ever around her and that you're ruining any chance she has of being asked out." Laura stopped in the doorway, and he took in the smile that touched the edges of her lips as he tried to figure out what she was talking about.

"I don't scare them. That's crazy. And who is this kid?"

This time, his wife did laugh. "Oh, my darling husband, you have a way about you whenever a boy gets near your daughter. Just the way you look at them, you let them know that they're not good enough for her and that if they do anything inappropriate, you'll seriously hurt them. You did it with Chelsea, and now Sarah. So I'm just saying, ease up."

Then Laura stepped out of the kitchen, and he was left alone with the remnants of breakfast, seeing the bus still driving away in the distance and hearing Brandon crying again. He could feel the angst of having to deal with yet another boy who would come calling and wanting to take his daughter out.

There were days he wondered if everyone was testing him.

Chapter 2

"You got a second?" Andy said as he slapped Jeremy's shoulder.

Jeremy stood staring at the engine of his truck, seeing the oil was way down again. He was going to have to do something, because it was starting to run pretty rough, and he could smell something burning. Then there was the transmission fluid and the brakes, which were close to shot, and he knew he needed new pads. The cold was setting in, and he'd had to get a boost just the day before because the engine wouldn't start. It seemed as if everything was piling on him from everywhere.

He took a breath, watching it mist in the cold, and said nothing as he leaned on the truck. His dad was looking at the dirty engine, wearing his black winter coat, his hands shoved in his pockets.

"You have something on your mind?" Jeremy said and picked up the wrench on the lip of the engine block, then tossed it into the old second-hand toolbox his dad had given him.

"I do. Wanted to have a chat with you about some things." His dad lifted his chin toward the truck. "Seems you've been spending a lot of time patching this truck. May be time to look at something else."

Was his dad kidding? He was feeling the stress of everything, which had only grown since he received his latest paycheck from the hardware store, which wasn't going to get him rich anytime soon. He and Tiffy would likely be living paycheck to paycheck, and that was if he could find something reasonable for them to rent. He now had a son, food to buy, and everything else that went with a family. He pulled in another breath, and this time he felt the ache build in his chest, feeling the cold scrape deep in his lungs.

"No, this will get me by," he replied. "I'm not spending anything else. What is it you want?" The minute he said it, he could tell by his dad's expression that he'd taken it wrong. He closed the hood with a clunk and took in the grease on his hands.

"Well, seems that this would be a start," Andy said. "Not sure what's going on with you. Your mom and I have stayed out of your business, even after you moved Tiffy and Brandon in and surprised all of us with this impending wedding, which neither you nor Tiffy have said one word about lately. Christmas is coming, just around the corner. I guess I'm kind of wondering if this wedding is still a go, or maybe you realized you've jumped the gun."

There it was. He pulled in another breath and wondered if his dad had ever felt anything of what he was feeling. Then there was school and the exams he'd just finished, the final essays he'd stayed up late to get done the night before. There would be a few weeks' break, and then he'd have to start again in January when right now what he needed was to earn his way in the world. He glanced over to the house, seeing the smoke from the chimney. It always looked so warm and inviting against the snow-covered ground, and he could see the winter sun disappearing. In another hour, it would be dark.

"We can't stay here forever," Jeremy said. "I just didn't realize that there isn't enough."

The way his dad looked at him, he could see he may still have been taking it the wrong way—or maybe the right way. He didn't know. He shrugged.

"I don't know," he said. "It's just everything seems to be sitting on my shoulders, and I feel as if any decision I make is the wrong one. Do you have any idea what it costs for a place, and then food, groceries, this damn heap of a truck that needs more and more work? And then my job is just part time. It's not enough to cover everything. I don't know if I can do it. I wake up in the morning, and instead of the excitement I used to have, being with Tiffy right after I proposed, right after I had her move in, I'm now worrying. Do you know I actually puked yesterday?" He pressed his hand to the back of his neck and squeezed, pulling his cold hand roughly across it.

This time his dad glanced away, and he opened his mouth to say something. When he looked back, Jeremy realized how strong his dad was. He looked after all of them, made decisions for all of them, and he made it seem so effortless. Easy. How could he have thought he could do this and be the man his father was?

"Hey, you listen here," Andy said, then rested his hand on Jeremy's shoulder and squeezed. "No one said you need to rush out and get a place, so you can get that out of your head. I know Tiffy's working, too. She's got that job in town at that new health food store. I'm sure it's not much, but…"

Jeremy wasn't sure what else his dad was going to say. "You forget she makes less than I do. Minimum wage buys you nothing. I promised Tiffy we'd get a place. Regardless, we can't stay here forever. I think in the new year I'm going to quit school, pick up full-time work." *And ask for more money.*

His dad shoved his hands in his pockets. "That's pretty hasty, Jeremy. So you quit school and work full time at the hardware store, and then what? Because it sounds to me as if you're thinking you need to take on everything. Is that why you're so stressed? We see it, your mom and me, and then there's this tension between you and Tiffy, which is now making its way down to your son. You aren't on the same page. You quitting school, working full time, and moving into some tiny apartment with the way everything is between you and Tiffy right now is exactly what you shouldn't do. It would ensure this thing between you two doesn't work out."

"Tiffy and Brandon are my responsibility," Jeremy said, pulling a rag from his jacket pocket and wiping at the grease on his hands. Then he tossed it too into the tool box on the ground.

"Never said they weren't, just saying that you might be overthinking things. And you didn't answer me about the wedding. Getting married was all you wanted a few weeks ago, and now is it on the back burner? If it is, that's fine. You don't have to get married. We don't live in a time where having a kid equals marriage because society will tar and feather you otherwise. No one cares anymore whether you're married, divorced, living together. They don't even ask, and Brandon certainly won't care. What he will care about is whether his mom and dad are at each other's throats, arguing."

Jeremy took in the way his dad was trying to figure him

out. He wasn't sure when he and Tiffy had stopped talking about the wedding. She was the one who'd wanted it, but at the same time, it was something he had wanted, as well. He didn't know why. It would be symbolic, just to say she was his, his wife, with his name. His.

He pulled in another breath. "You don't get it," he snapped before hearing a car and turning his head, spotting Tiffy behind the wheel of the brown Volvo, driving in over the plowed dirt driveway. He should've wanted to go to her, pull her out of the car, kiss her, but he couldn't get past the distance that had found its way between them. Why and when had it happened?

"Well then explain it to me," Andy said, "because I'm trying, Jeremy. This here with you and the way you're reacting, I don't know what to make of it. Seeing this tension between you and Tiffy, and you not hearing her and deciding all of a sudden that you can say and do whatever you want with your son, who seems to know how to get anything he wants from you… Giving in may seem like it's easier, but it'll create more obstacles and problems down the road. You're teaching him that he can have whatever he wants, and by not creating a united front with Tiffy, who, might I add, has been raising him alone until now and has done a fine job, you're not setting boundaries that he very much needs. Dismissing what Tiffy says to him as if it doesn't matter is going to cause a heap of trouble for you, for him, and especially for Tiffy."

He could feel his shoulders tighten and took in Tiffy, who stepped out of her mom's old car and closed the door with her hip. She just stared at him. He should've been hurrying over to her, but instead he was wondering why his dad was even bringing up Brandon. Yeah, okay, this morning had been an issue, but he was tired, and Tiffy had slipped into the shower before him, and Brandon was hungry. He was just trying to make it easier on all of them, and he didn't know what to say.

"It's just too much," Jeremy snapped. "I never expected all this."

His dad squeezed his shoulder, then pulled his hand away and shook his head, stepping back.

Tiffy had started walking their way.

"Hi, Tiffy," Andy called. "How was work?"

It was exactly what he should have said, and he didn't miss the way his dad's expression softened as he offered Tiffy a smile. She was beautiful, her gray winter coat zipped up and a cream wool hat pulled over her dark hair. His dad and mom both had a soft spot for her.

"Busy, but it's a job," she said.

Andy nodded. "Look, I think you two need to talk, work some things out." He glanced back to Jeremy with his icy blue eyes, and he had the feeling his dad wanted to also add to him, *Pull your shit together*. But he didn't. "Brandon is down for a nap. Laura and I will keep an ear out for him, so you two take your time."

Then his dad started back to the house, and that left him and Tiffy in the cold. Neither of them could use Brandon for an excuse.

"So what is it your dad seems to think we need to work out?" Tiffy pulled her hands from her pockets and crossed them over her chest.

He flicked his gaze to the house, seeing his dad in the kitchen window, talking with his mom. He realized how much he'd taken for granted, because they made everything look so easy. He pulled his gaze back to Tiffy, who stared at him, expecting…what? Nothing good, he supposed.

"The wedding," he said. "We need to talk about getting

married, Brandon, where we're going to live—and I'm going to quit school."

He waited for her to say something, but instead she blinked and shook her head. Then she just turned and started walking toward the house.

Chapter 3

"Wait, what are you doing?" Jeremy said. "I'm trying to have a conversation here with you, and you walk away?"

She didn't like his tone. In fact, there was so much about him lately that had her feeling as if he regretted everything about her, her being there, and the fact that his ring was on her finger. Maybe this was his way of trying to make her go away and break this off. His hand was now on her shoulder, and he somehow had her stopped and turned around. She took in the fire in his eyes, those green eyes that had a way of completely unsettling her and making her give in when she needed to stand her ground.

"Sounds to me like you're telling me what you want, like it's already decided," she said, then pulled the ring off her finger. "So how about this? No wedding. You're off the hook, no hard feelings." She held it out to him, and he just stared at it before slipping it back on her finger.

"Don't be ridiculous," he said. "We're getting married. Stop trying to push me away."

How did he do that?

"I don't understand you, Jeremy," she said. "Now you're talking about quitting school. You think I want that on me? One day you'll blame me for your choice to give up your education and your opportunity for a better future. I didn't have that option, but I would give anything to go back to school and finish. I was really good in school, and yet I did it for Brandon and would do it again, even though I will likely only ever have the kind of jobs I never pictured myself doing, minimum-wage service work. You got to finish high school and go on to post-secondary, and there's no way I want to be responsible for you quitting, giving it all up. You would look at me and blame me, thinking you could've had so much more if it weren't for me. And yes, let's talk about Brandon and how you seem to be undermining me all the time. You give him everything and anything he wants. I say no, you say yes. Do you not get how hard it is to be a parent as it is, and then you go and just give in?"

He made a face and went to step back, and she thought maybe he was getting ready to argue, disagree, or maybe just dismiss her. "So it's about this morning and his break-fast," he said. "You could've been the one to feed him, you know. I was up most of the night finishing up a paper that was supposed to be handed in days ago, before the winter break. This morning, you were in the shower, and Brandon was hungry and calling for you."

"And so what, you feed him sugar and crap because he won't eat anything else? You give him a bowl of cereal. You tell him no. You be a parent. Stop giving in to a little kid who's suddenly figured out how to get you to do anything." She realized she was getting loud, and the smile that touched his lips was anything but happy.

"Then you start getting up with him," he said. "I think

we need to start setting some ground rules here on who's doing what."

She just stared at him. She couldn't believe he'd said that. "Oh, and tell me what you think these rules should be."

The screen door squeaked behind her, and she took in the way Jeremy glanced over her shoulder to whoever was there and then back to her.

"Well," he said, "I'll be working full time at the hardware store if I can get more hours and more money. If not, I'll find something else. You're going to have to pick up more of the slack with Brandon. You're his mother. My mother did it. My dad had this place to run, so my mom handled all the cooking, the cleaning. She looked after all of us, and as far as a place goes…"

She lifted the flat of her hand. "Whoa, wait. Stop just a minute, there. Did you seriously just say to me that because I'm a woman, you expect me to look after Brandon? That your mom is a stay-home mom and did all the cooking and cleaning, and your dad did nothing, and that you somehow expect me to slip into that role? Is that what you mean about picking up the slack, that I don't do enough? And did you seriously just insinuate that because you work full time, I'm to look after the home front after I work my own full-time job? That evidently doesn't seem to count in your mind. I also suppose that you expect to work, come home, and not lift a finger or do anything, because a woman's place is in the kitchen, the bedroom, and waiting on a man."

For a second, she thought he stopped breathing. She heard his dad clear his throat behind her.

"And maybe in this little talk about ground rules," she continued, "you were about to add that you expect me to work my own pitiful full-time job and look after Brandon, all the while cooking, cleaning, and looking after the home and you, picking up after you, not talking back, doing what you say, because you set and establish the rules—and I'm just a woman."

"Uh…that wasn't what I meant." Jeremy lifted his brows, and she found herself fisting her hands. She could hear the porch squeak behind her, but she couldn't pull her gaze from him.

"Really? Because it sounded to me as if you were about to say how little importance my job has. Or did you forget that I work as well? I know it's likely not at the same level of importance as the hardware store, and I'm just a lowly clerk, easily replaceable. Oh, wait! You are too, but of course, you being male, and a white male, at that, you likely make double what I do for an equivalent job, so I guess that really does make you of more importance, doesn't it?"

She leaned in, but this time she felt a hand touch her shoulder, and Andy stepped down beside her. Anger was pulsing through her, making her claw for another breath. The expression on his face was priceless, but mad was mad, and Jeremy had managed to push every one of her buttons.

"How about I stop this before it goes any further and neither of you is able to yank out the foot you've jammed in your mouth?" Andy said.

Jeremy actually shut his eyes and gave his head a shake. When he opened them, he stared at Tiffy as if she'd lost her mind. "That wasn't what I was saying. Shit, Tiffy, what the hell is with you? I was just…"

"Stop," Andy said, "and let's table this thing about equality. That argument has already been fought and won and settled."

"Well, actually, it hasn't, considering men still make

more than women," Tiffy said. What was wrong with her? She just couldn't help herself. "I believe it's something like for every dollar a man earns, a woman is paid eighty cents, but then if you really get into the nitty gritty of the stats, depending on where you are in the country, Asian women have the smallest wage gap with white men, coming in at eighty-seven cents, while white women are at seventy-nine cents, black women at sixty-three cents, and Hispanic women at fifty-four cents. And then let's not forget how women with children today are still penalized in the work force, while men are rewarded, and women's earnings decrease with age, yet men's keep increasing." She pulled in a breath.

Andy and Jeremy both stared at her. It was just that she was a stickler for facts, statistics, and numbers, because they showed what was wrong in a clear, no-nonsense way that no one could argue with.

"Well, I had no idea" was all Andy said.

Jeremy made a face as if he didn't get it and she was being ridiculous.

"So how about we table all of this," Andy continued, "and you can both come inside, because Laura and I want to talk to you about something."

Jeremy was still staring at her, and she knew he didn't have a clue what to say.

"Tiffy, Jeremy," Andy added again, and she pulled her gaze from Jeremy, taking in his father, who was waiting for her to move, to do something.

"Fine," she said and took in the way Jeremy inclined his head, although she was positive they could still go another round or two. If she told anyone how much she enjoyed sparring with Jeremy and not giving in to any of his ridiculous demands, she knew they would think she was crazy.

Chapter 4

He slipped off his coat and had just hung it on a hook when his mom grabbed his ear and yanked.

"Ow, ow, Mom, seriously, what the hell are you doing?" He didn't know how she did it, but she managed to drag him into the kitchen, his head angled and pulled down. He felt like an absolute idiot, considering how big and strong he was, and she was basically five-two and didn't weigh more than a hundred and thirty pounds, give or take.

"Are you kidding me, Jeremy?" Laura said. "I can't believe you said what you did. You really think so little of me and your dad that you somehow think your dad made me stay home, that he shoved me into this kitchen and had me wiping snotty noses and picking up after you because I'm a woman? I chose this because I loved you guys, but right now, I swear I want to smack you silly!"

His mom let go of his ear, and his hand went right there, feeling the sting and seeing both his dad and Tiffy standing side by side in the kitchen, on the other side of the island, staring at him and then his mom. Neither of them said a word, but the expressions on their faces showed they were as stunned as he was by what his mom had done. It would be funny, he thought, if his ear weren't still smarting from how hard his mom had yanked it. He took in her green eyes, which were shooting sparks his way.

No one said anything.

No one dared to say anything.

"It may have come out wrong, and…" he started to say, but his dad raised a brow as if waiting for him to shove his other foot in his mouth. Andy didn't seem too inclined to help him out, and Tiffy was now staring at his mom.

Jeremy didn't know how to tell his mom that her being there at home, raising them, had been something he realized now, in this second, that he'd taken for granted.

"Really? Because your dad and I could hear you outside, and I'm pretty sure the words you used were 'ground rules,' saying Tiffy would need to look after Brandon because your work and your job is of more importance. I cannot believe I raised a son who's so dense. Let me also point out to you, because you seem to have missed this fact, that Tiffy is the one who raised Brandon all alone until now, not you. And who said anything about you having to quit school? Marriage or no marriage, you two have a son, and you're living here. Yes, you need your own space, your own place, but this ranch is more than big enough. So we're bringing in a contractor and turning the loft in the barn into your home, your apartment. It will be yours, your space, your place." His mom was spitting mad still, but he was now stuck on the barn, the loft.

"That's really generous, but…" Tiffy started from beside his dad, who was still staring his way, shaking his head.

"You're family," Andy said, "and it seems the stress of a

job, and school, and money is taking its toll on your reasoning, both of you. Besides, having Brandon here and raising him here so we can help out is a better option. This is a big place, with a lot of land."

He didn't know what to say to dig his way out of the doghouse he seemed to continually be in with his mom. "I'm not a chauvinist," Jeremy added with effect, but he didn't miss the way his mom shifted her gaze to the ceiling and let out a huff as she walked around him to the fridge, where she pulled out two large packages of chicken legs and rested them on the counter.

His dad shifted his gaze to his mom, and he saw the protectiveness in the way he looked at her. He knew this about his dad, but seeing the motion now, he realized it was so much more.

Laura turned around and crossed her arms, giving him that pissed-off mom look again. "You just have a lot to learn about opening your mouth," she said. "And for the record, Jeremy, your dad never once told me to stay home. I didn't even get to finish high school because of what happened with Gabriel, but your dad encouraged me to take classes and get my diploma, and he always stepped in and helped with all of you to make it happen. You think he ever said to me that I had to stay home, that there were rules, that he was too busy to raise any of you, to change a dirty diaper, to play with you, to talk to you, to father you?"

He looked to his dad again, who was now leaning against the sink.

"I'm sorry," Jeremy said. "It came out wrong. Mom, Tiffy..." He looked at both of them, wishing he could figure out how to keep from saying the wrong thing. He didn't miss the hint of a smile that Tiffy tried to hide. His mom, though, merely glanced his way, her gaze long and lingering before it fell on his dad.

"Andy, you need to get going and pick up Sarah," she said and gestured to the door.

"Right. You need anything in town?" Andy asked before he walked over and leaned down to kiss his mom on the lips she offered to him.

"No, but thanks."

Then his dad stepped away, closer to where he stood on the opposite side of the island as Tiffy. "As your mom said, you don't need to look for a place, because the loft in the barn will be yours. I'll call the contractor tomorrow and get him out here, so you both can stop worrying about a place to rent and having that added expense. And you'll finish school. Forget the full-time work. Both of you need to sit down and decide if you're getting married. As I said, it's not necessary, and maybe, considering all of this discord, you should wait." His dad's gaze lingered for a minute, and then he stepped away, reaching for the keys on a hook by the back door. He tossed Jeremy one last look and then left.

"Can I help with dinner?" Tiffy said to his mom, but her gaze didn't leave Jeremy.

"Sure, it would help if you could grab the bag of potatoes from the pantry and peel them."

He just stood there, seeing his mom's back as she reached into the cupboard and pulled out a roaster, then resting it on the island. Her eyes landed on Jeremy, and he wondered how his mom could make him feel as if he were just a kid. "You know what?" he said. "I can make dinner, me and Tiffy. Give you a break, since you're in here every night, cooking for all of us."

What was he doing? He hated cooking.

A bright smile touched his mom's lips, and her eyes lit up. "Trying to dig your way out of the dog house?" she teased and then glanced over her shoulder to Tiffy. "You know what? I'm going to take you both up on this, since you also need to talk. With a place to live now taken off your list of worries, you both can talk about the one thing you're avoiding. As your dad said, it doesn't matter to us whether you get married or not. Just figure it out—and make sure you season the chicken before you put it in the oven. Make a salad, and steam some broccoli and carrots. Boil the potatoes and mash them. Oh, and Brandon is still sleeping. He's been down for a couple hours. Zach is in his room, doing homework. I'm going to read a book."

Laura walked out of the kitchen, and Jeremy stared at the two family packs of chicken legs, seeing another expense. He glanced to Tiffy's back as she peeled potatoes, then walked over to her and stood beside her, taking hold of one of the packages of chicken legs and ripping it open, trying to remember what his mom had done to make them taste so good.

"So let's talk wedding," Jeremy said. "The gift from my parents, the loft in the barn…and I didn't mean to say that because you're a woman, you get to pick up the slack and I set the rules. What I meant to say was that I was up most of the night finishing an essay that was overdue, and I was tired and had only a few hours' sleep. It was more about establishing order for both of us. I'm sorry about your job. I never meant to imply it was of no importance, because it is, and you should finish high school. You should take classes now."

Tiffy was staring down at the potato in her hand. She'd stopped peeling.

"I didn't realize, too, that I was giving in to Brandon…"

Tiffy tossed the potato in the sink and turned to face him. He could see he was about to get another earful, so he pressed his finger to her lips.

"Let me finish before you strap me to the stake and roast me for not understanding. You've always been smart, way smarter than me, and you've got a mouth on you. I never know when you're going to rattle off facts I would never have a clue about, but if you could just let me finish and get out what I'm trying to say…" He pulled his hand away.

It took a second, but she seemed to back down. She nodded, but this time she didn't say anything.

"I wasn't trying to undermine you with Brandon. I didn't even think it was a big deal about the Nutella…"

"And bedtime, and skipping his bath, and putting away his toys," she cut in, and he stared at her, wondering what she was talking about. Maybe his confusion showed, as she shrugged and then rolled her eyes. "You don't even remember, do you?"

What could he say? Being a father wasn't something he'd expected at this age, and he was at a loss to remember what he'd done that was so wrong.

"When I tell Brandon it's bedtime and you say, 'Oh, it's okay, he can stay up a little longer,' or you say to him, 'Hey, bud, let's go check out the pony,' but he's got his toys all spread out, and when I tell him he has to put them all back in the bin first, you say he can do it later, and then there was two nights ago, when I called him for his bath, and he went running to you, saying he didn't want a bath, and you said—"

"That he didn't have to have one," he finished. Now he remembered, but it hadn't been the way Tiffy implied. "Sorry is all I can say. I never realized what I did that was…thoughtless," he added.

She watched him, and he could see she was trying to figure him out. "Maybe your mom and dad are right, and we shouldn't get married." She had one hand on her hip and was looking up at him, her face perfect and round, her lips pursed. He knew she was giving him an out.

He leaned down and pressed a kiss to her lips before a pair of little arms grabbed his leg.

"Daddy!" Brandon was all smiles, wearing just a pull-up diaper. "Hungry! Nutella!" He was bouncing on his toes, and Tiffy said nothing.

"Yeah, no," Jeremy said. "Never again, little man. Your mommy and daddy are making chicken." He lifted Brandon in his arms and took in the packages of chicken.

"No chicken!" Brandon demanded, and Jeremy took in his frown.

"Sorry, bud, not a choice. It's chicken or nothing." He felt his son's bulky diaper and saw the way Tiffy raised her brow. "Why don't I change Brandon, clean him up, and, uh…" He gestured to the chicken with his other hand. "I don't have a clue how to season that chicken. My mom always made everything look so easy."

"You change him," Tiffy said. "I'll do the chicken, and you can make the salad."

He took in Brandon, whom he expected to put up a fuss, but he was just looking from his mommy to his daddy. "Deal," he said and leaned in to kiss Tiffy again. Then he stepped back, taking in Tiffy as she reached for the chicken and ripped open the package. "What about a new year wedding?"

She stilled and turned around, her hands resting on the counter behind her. Evidently, she hadn't expected that. "You sure?" she asked.

"Yeah, more than you know."

She seemed to consider, glancing down at her hand and over to Brandon. "You really think we can do it?"

He glanced out the window to the barn, for the first

time seeing something that seemed so right. "I know we can."

Chapter 5

Andy had five children, Gabriel, Chelsea, Jeremy, Sarah, and Zach, and he loved them more than he'd thought it was possible to love anyone. It was a love that was more than him, and he knew that when he was Jeremy's age, he could never have understood what it meant to be a father.

Then there was his wife, whom he loved more now than he'd thought was ever possible. She was the center of his world, his children's world, all of their worlds, and the only woman who could get him to see reason about anything, which was why he was walking through the hallway of the school and doing his best not to snarl at any of the jocks and seniors who were still lingering there, doing what guys that age did.

He had to remind himself that they weren't all dead-beat losers just waiting for the opportunity to put their hands on his daughter. Then he heard her, her laughter, as he approached the library, his hands shoved in his pockets. He stepped inside.

She'd always had the kind of laugh that he wished he

could bottle and have on hand to listen to anytime he had a shitty day. It was genuine and uplifting, starting at her toes and going right through her, never forced or artificial. Her back was to him, and he took in the tank she was wearing, having taken off the blouse she'd worn that morning. There were boxes on the tables, filled with stuff, and the boy in front of her was tall, thin, with light brown styled hair. He was giving everything to her with a smile that was far too friendly.

Andy could feel his hands fisting in his pockets as his eyes latched on to the boy, who was standing far too close to his daughter. Everything about his body language said he wanted her. Andy cleared his throat, and they both turned. He didn't miss how they were the only two there. Like, where were the teachers, the adults?

"Dad, hi! We were just finishing up," Sarah said, watching him. He could see the way her expression changed as if she thought he was going to say or do something that would…what, embarrass her?

"Take your time. I'll wait," he said. "And this is…?" He stepped closer and took in the way the boy suddenly stood straighter. His smile slipped, and he could hear his wife in his head, telling him to ease up. Yes, he could have offered him a smile instead of staring at him, letting him know that he could and would make his life a living hell if he touched his daughter, disrespected her, or basically continued to ogle her the way he had been. Yeah, Sarah was the spitting image of her mother, blond, gorgeous— and his daughter.

He took another step, seeing the sweat pop up on the boy's brow as he continued to stare down at him as if he were something he'd wiped from the bottom of his feet.

"This is Reese, Dad. Did Mom talk to you?" Sarah added, and he took in her confusion, knowing he was supposed to lay off the intimidation, but right now it was beyond him to give any guy a pass with his kid.

"Yeah, she did," he replied. "So, Reese, how old are you?"

He didn't miss the way the kid damn near crapped his pants. He really shouldn't be enjoying this as much as he was.

"Seventeen. Uh…"

"Mr. Friessen," Andy added, as he saw the kid was having trouble with how to address him. "So you're in the same grade as my daughter, same classes?"

Reese glanced once to Sarah, and he wondered if the kid was expecting her to help him out.

"Yes, Dad," she said. "Reese and I are in English together."

He'd let her answer for him, which said a lot.

"What are your plans after high school?" Andy continued. "What do you have planned for your future?"

Sarah had now reached for her blouse, which was hanging over the back of the chair, and slipped it on. She was shrugging on her blue coat, as well, and the boy was shifting his glance from her to Andy, his hands now shoved in his baggy jeans pockets.

"Not sure yet. I'm thinking about trade school, maybe working as a contractor. My parents, though, want me to get a degree in business or the medical field. Neither interests me, but I have time to decide." He bounced on the balls of his feet and glanced to the door.

Of course, he'd made the kid nervous. He knew Reese was looking for the opportunity to slip away. He should really just let him, but at the same time, this was his daughter.

"You think so, do you?" he stated, knowing his tone was only adding to the kid's nerves.

"I should…" Reese gestured to the door.

Andy gestured with his head. "Go," he said, and Reese didn't wait another second: He was gone out the door. Andy took in the way Sarah looked up at him as she lifted a scarf around her neck. She wasn't impressed. "What?" He shrugged.

"Mom said she would talk to you, Dad. That wasn't nice, what you just did. You scared him away." She reached for her backpack and lifted it from the chair beside her, and Andy stepped closer to his daughter and took it from her.

"I'm sorry," he said. "Yes, your mom did talk to me, and I tried, but I love you, my little girl, and that's beyond me."

She shook her head and gestured in the air. "I'm never going to be asked out! That isn't fair, Dad. We weren't doing anything wrong."

Did she have any idea what she was saying? He'd been her age, Reese's age. He knew exactly what he was thinking, and there was nothing innocent about the way his daughter was dressed and openly flirting with him.

"Hey, you listen to me. You're my daughter, and I love you, but if you think me coming in here and adding some heat can scare off a guy as easy as that, ask yourself if that guy is really good enough for you. You're so special, and when you meet the right guy, you're going to know he's the right guy because he won't let me intimidate him or chase him away. He'll have a voice, he'll stand up for you. He won't run when it gets a little too uncomfortable." And Andy would breathe a lot easier knowing his daughter would be with a guy who was worthy of her, though he hoped that would come a long way down the road.

She just stared at him, and he knew she didn't get it.

"Okay, I'll ease up," he said, and she offered him that

smile that could get him to do anything—almost.

"Really, you promise?"

He squeezed the strap of the backpack and then stepped closer, sliding his other hand under his daughter's chin before touching the side of her hair, and he slid his hand over her shoulder and had her walking with him to the door. "To a point, but by no means will I give any guy a pass. I'm your father. Anyone wants to take you out, they come to the door." He'd make sure the boys understood clearly that they'd better think twice before letting their teenage hormones get the better of them.

"That doesn't sound like you're going to ease up, Dad. Could you not have offered a smile, been a little nicer?"

He was walking down the now empty hall to the front door, knowing what his daughter wanted him to say. Nicer? He didn't know how he'd pull that off. "I'll try. That's all I can promise you," he said and took in the way his daughter frowned as she glanced up to him and shook her head.

"Oh, Dad, I'm not going to break, and I do have a good head on my shoulders. After all, I have you and Mom as parents."

Now what was he supposed to say to that? He'd silently feared this day would come.

"You always did know the right thing to say," he replied as he pushed open the door, and they stepped out under the dark winter sky. He could see his breath in the Montana cold.

"Well, I learned everything from you, Dad," she said in her teasing way, and he wished he could lock her away and keep every guy from her, but he couldn't.

Any day now, they would all start knocking on the door, and when they did, he'd likely be completely gray and short-tempered, and his wife would be there, reminding him every time to ease up.

Chapter 6

Christmas had been a madhouse, with gifts that stretched out two feet from the tree and surrounded it. Tiffy's parents and her brother, Alex, had all come out to the ranch, and Chelsea and Ric had come home from Boston and were staying in Chelsea's old room. They had announced to everyone on Christmas morning that they were planning on an April wedding at the ranch, nothing big, family only.

Elizabeth and Gabriel had also joined in, announcing how Gabriel had convinced Elizabeth that marriage wasn't the worst idea ever. Tiffy still smiled, thinking of how everyone had laughed. She realized there was a joke in there somewhere, only she didn't have a clue what it was. Needless to say, they were talking summer, July, and then everyone had shifted their attention to her and Jeremy, putting everything into the plans for their New Year's Day wedding.

Even the construction on their new place had started with a fury over the holidays. There was a full crew and enough noise to drive a sane person crazy, and in three to four weeks, they would have their own place and would be moving out of the main house, where they were still living with Jeremy's parents, into something that was theirs.

Now, she took in her image in the full-length mirror in Andy and Laura's master suite, seeing her mom behind her in a blue dress that was both flattering and fun, and Laura in a deep green dress that showed off her amazing figure. Both wore priceless expressions as they stared at her in her white silk taffeta wedding gown with a high slit up the side, off-the-shoulder sleeves, and a low cut showing off her amazing cleavage.

"You're absolutely beautiful. I think I'm going to start crying again," her mom, Flo, said and dabbed at her eyes. Even Laura's green eyes appeared to mist a bit.

"You're gorgeous, Tiffy, and Jeremy is so lucky. I wish both of you years and years of happiness and more." Laura slid her hand over Tiffy's shoulder.

"Wait! There's the veil," Sarah said from where she stood to the side, wearing a full-length satin peach gown that was identical to Chelsea's and showed what sexy, attractive women the Friessen daughters were. Sarah and Chelsea lifted the fine lace of the veil and attached it to the back of her hair, which was pinned up. She had to force herself to pull in a breath, feeling like a princess. She wondered if this was how every bride felt. She thought she could stand there all day, taking in her image, never having felt this beautiful.

Then Chelsea, with her dark hair, and Sarah, with her blond, each on either side of her, slid their arms around her and sandwiched her between them. "My brother is one lucky guy," Sarah said.

"And that nephew of mine reminds me so much of

Jeremy, a ball of energy and tons of fun," Chelsea added. She had Jeremy's smile, she realized.

There was another tap on the door. They all turned as her mom stepped over and opened it. It was her dad, Wayne, wearing a dark suit and a warm smile.

"Jeremy was wondering if you're ready yet. Actually, I think he's a little worried you changed your mind and have climbed out the window. The pastor is here, and everyone is ready. Your brother just arrived, and he and Ric have each poured a double scotch."

Everyone looked at her.

"Yup, let's do this," she said and turned to Chelsea and Sarah. She was just getting to know Jeremy's twin, who spoke his language and translated it well for her, and Sarah, who offered her an easy smile and gentle encouragement and who seemed to know whenever she was reaching her wits' end with her brother. Yup, she was getting two great sisters out of the deal.

"Lead the way, girls," she said.

Sarah left first, and then Chelsea followed with Laura. Tiffy took her dad's proffered arm and then her mom's, sandwiched between them in the hallway, listening to the soft music playing as she walked arm in arm with them to the living room, which was decorated with all manner of Christmas bows and ribbons, the huge tree still in the window.

Jeremy was standing with Zach and Gabriel before the pastor, a dark-haired man with glasses and a smile. Her mom and dad stopped in front of Jeremy, and she kissed them both before she took Jeremy's arm and let her gaze land on Alex. He took in Jeremy and then her.

"You sure about this?" was all he said, holding what she realized was a tumbler of scotch.

"I am," she added, and Alex leaned in and kissed her cheek before tossing Jeremy a "Don't screw it up" look.

Then she married Jeremy Friessen under the mistletoe.

He was the man she'd crushed on, fallen in love with, had a child with, and now would build a life with.

Whatever came their way, she realized they could handle it—together.

Turn the page for a sneak peek of
A REASON TO BREATHE the next book in THE FRIESSENS
Available in print, eBook & audio

A Reason to Breathe

Everyone knows the first time you meet that special some-one: Your eyes connect from across the room, and you smile and work up the courage to say hello. It's a simple feat for most people, but not for Trevor Friessen, who struggles to fit into this world and thinks he always will—that is, until he meets a girl who is as different from him as she is the same.

"Our families and everyone around us, what they don't understand is that we too feel love."

A Reason to Breathe

CHAPTER 1

His sister Katy wore an odd expression, sitting at the kitchen table alone, staring at seven papers. She'd ripped the staple out of them, and it now lay on the table beside an almost empty bowl with a spoon sticking out. There was milk spilled beside it. How could she not see that? It was so close to her arm that if she moved, it would be in the milk, and that wouldn't be good because then she'd have to change her shirt, which was already wrinkled.

"Why are you standing behind me, Trevor?" She didn't look up right away, but he watched as she put down the papers, scattering them on the table in a mess instead of straightening them in a pile. He could see the milk still there. She was about to put her arm in it as she rested it on the table and turned to face him.

"Aren't you going to clean that up?" he said. He had on his favorite jeans, black ones, and his favorite black super-hero shirt, Captain America. Katy was wearing a faded orange shirt with lines and squiggles. He didn't like the lines and squiggles, and the color orange was annoying. It was the one shirt he wished she'd put in the garbage. Maybe he'd do it for her.

"Trevor, seriously, dude, you need to get a life. Aren't you supposed to be out helping Dad today with the cows or something?"

Katy pushed the papers aside and scraped back her chair, then picked up her bowl and put it in the dishwasher. She left the spilled milk and the papers, and he cleared his throat before he felt her hand on his shoulder. He had to force himself to look her way, knowing she'd stay there until he did. His mom and dad, Katy, Steven, and his sister Becky always said over and over for him to look at them, and it was frankly annoying. Right now there was a thread hanging off her shirt sleeve that she also needed to take care of.

"Trevor, you didn't answer me, and you're doing that throat-clearing thing again that's really annoying. Did you eat breakfast yet? What are you doing today?"

Her shirt collar was folded correctly on one side but sticking up on the other. He reached over and grabbed the edge of her collar and unfolded it so it sat perfectly just like the other side. "I'm working today," he said.

He realized Katy was frowning now. Why? Her hair was pulled back in a high ponytail. At least she wasn't sad anymore.

"Did you seriously just fix my collar?" she said. She didn't say thank you. She really should say thank you.

"You look better now, but I don't like your shirt. You should change. It's ugly."

She just shook her head. "Seriously, Trevor. Tell me how you really feel."

Well, he didn't like it. He'd just told her that. Maybe she hadn't heard him. Then she reached over and rustled his dark hair, which was short and neatly combed.

"Hey," he said, and all she did was laugh as if it was funny before she walked around him and picked up the papers in one hand so they were crumpled, not even taking the time to tidy them up so they were neat and together. He reached up and tidied his hair, but he was going to have to go back upstairs to fix it properly.

"Where are you working?" Katy said. "Is this the job Mom and Dad were talking about?" She wasn't looking at him anymore but at those papers again. He wished she'd straighten them instead of holding them in the mess they were in. "Trevor, I asked you a question."

About what again?

"Huh?" he said, smoothing his hand over his hair.

She tapped her fingers on the counter. "The job, Trevor. Tell me where you're working today and what you're doing."

"The grocery store. I'm working in the bakery department. I get to package cookies, make boxes…" And the broken ones he got to put aside and eat later, but he wasn't going to share that part. That was enough sharing—especially since she was ignoring the mess on the table. He walked to the sink, picked up the sponge, and strode to the table to wipe the spot of milk, and then there were the crumbs.

"Mister OCD," she said. "Seriously, Trevor?"

He took in his sister and his mom, who appeared distracted as she walked into the kitchen, poured a coffee, and looked from him to Katy.

"What's going on?" Emily asked. She was looking at Katy, so maybe he could leave now and fix his hair and then read the new *Adventures of Tintin* book he'd picked up at the library yesterday.

"Just Trevor being Trevor, the neat freak," Katy said.

"No, I'm not," he said. He couldn't figure out why she

was smiling and what the exchange was between her and their mom.

"Don't worry about it, Trevor. I'm just teasing you. What time do you have to leave for work?" Katy folded the papers, and his eyes went right there, seeing how uneven they were.

He glanced to the clock on the stove, seeing it was eight thirty-three.

"You start at nine, Trevor," his mom said. "Are you ready to go? I'll drive you to work, and don't forget Uncle Neil is picking you up today. You and him are going to…"

He knew his mom was still talking, but he didn't hear her as he took in the coffee she'd poured and the fridge she'd opened to pull out leftover ribs. Ah…that was what he should've packed. Ribs would be a great lunch instead of the tuna salad he'd made.

He heard the back door slap closed and saw his dad, who went right to his mom and leaned down and kissed her. She smiled and was happy. His dad always made her happy. He turned away, seeing that Katy was watching him again, and it made him twitchy when she looked at him that way. She was doing that a lot as of late. He took a step to the side, then turned and started walking to the stairs to fix his hair, read, and then…

"Trevor, answer me. Did you not hear me?" Emily said.

He took in his mom and dad watching him, and Katy too, who was giving him that annoyed big sister look she often did. He hadn't heard a word they'd said.

"Good, I'm good," he said, knowing it was likely they'd asked him how he was. If not, their faces would give him a clue in about a minute, and he'd use his other answer, which was "Time to go."

"You were off in your head, so try again," Emily said.

"What are you supposed to be doing at work today? Are you allowed to be slow and take your time?"

His dad was giving him that hard gaze, but at least his dad didn't talk as much as his mom and sister did, and then there was Becky. Jack was even better, as he said even less, just things like "Move over, my turn with the remote." Yeah, Jack was better than all of them. He and his brother could share space, enjoy a game, and...

"Nope, I'll be fast," he said. "Okay, time to go. Bye, Dad. Bye, Katy. Come on, Mom." He started walking out of the kitchen, seeing his backpack at the front door, where he'd already packed his lunch, and he stopped at the mirror to see that his hair was still a ruffled mess. He used his fingers to tidy it to the side again.

"Change of plans, Trevor." Katy walked up beside him and slapped his shoulder. Her shirt was hanging over her jeans in a messy look. She never tucked it in. She was carrying her baggy purse, the one with fringes on the side that were too long and needed to be cut back. "I'm driving you."

"What? No," he said, seeing that his mom and dad weren't there anymore, but Katy was. The smile on her face as she stood right in front of him had him wanting to take a step back, because she was worse than his mom— nagging, talking to him, and making him talk about the sequence of his day as if he didn't know what he was doing. He couldn't just do what he wanted to do.

"Mom...!" he called out.

"Go with Katy," Emily replied from the kitchen. She didn't appear in the doorway, so that was that.

"Fine," he said, and he pushed open the door and walked over to her Jeep before climbing into the passenger side, closing the door, and fastening his seatbelt. He settled his backpack in the back seat as he waited for his sister.

About the Author

"Lorhainne Eckhart is one of my go to authors when I want a guaranteed good book. So many twists and turns, but also so much love and such a strong sense of family."

(LORA W., REVIEWER)

New York Times & USA Today bestseller Lorhainne Eckhart is best known for writing Raw Relatable Real Romance where "Morals and family are running themes." As one fan calls her, she is the "Queen of the family saga." (aherman) writing "the ups and downs of what goes on within a family but also with some suspense, angst and of course a bit of romance thrown in for good measure."

Follow Lorhainne on Bookbub to receive alerts on New Releases and Sales and join her mailing list at Lorhainne-Eckhart.com for her Monday Blog, all book news, give-aways and FREE reads. With over 120 books, audiobooks, and multiple series published and available at all, retailers now translated into six languages. She is a multiple recipient of the Readers' Favorite Award for Suspense and Romance, and lives in the Pacific Northwest on an island, is the mother of three, her oldest has autism and she is an advocate for never giving up on your dreams.

"Lorhainne Eckhart has this uncanny way of just hitting the spot every time with her books."

(CAROLINE L., REVIEWER)

The O'Connells: *The O'Connells of Livingston, Montana are not your typical family. A riveting collection of stories surrounding the ups and downs of what goes on within a family but also with some suspense, angst and of course a bit of romance thrown in for good measure. "I thought I loved the Friessens, but I absolutely adore the O'Connell's. Each and every book has different genres of stories, but the one thing in common is how she is able to wrap it around the family, which is the heart of each story." (C. Logue)*

The Friessens: *An emotional big family romance series, the Friessen family siblings find their relationships tested, lay their hearts on the line, and discover lasting love! "Lorhainne Eckhart is one of my go to authors when I want* a guaranteed good book. So many twists and turns, but also so much love and such a strong sense of family." (Lora W., Reviewer)

The Parker Sisters: The Parker Sisters are a close-knit family, and like any other family they have their ups and downs. Eckhart has crafted another intense family drama… "The character development is outstanding, and the emotional investment is high…" (Aherman, Reviewer)

The McCabe Brothers: Join the five McCabe siblings on their journeys to the dark and dangerous side of love! An intense, exhilarating collection of romantic thrillers you won't want to miss. — "Eckhart has a new series that is definitely worth the read. The queen of the family saga started this series with a spin-off of her wildly successful Friessen series." From a Readers' Favorite award—winning author and "queen of the family saga" (Aherman)

Billy Jo McCabe Mystery: The social worker and the cop, an unlikely couple drawn together on a small, secluded Pacific Northwest island where nothing is as it seems. Protecting the innocent comes at a cost, and what seems to be a sleepy, quiet town is anything but.

Lorhainne loves to hear from her readers! You can connect with me at:
www.LorhainneEckhart.com
lorhainneeckhart.le@gmail.com

facebook.com/AuthorLorhainneEckhart

twitter.com/LEckhart

instagram.com/lorhainneeckhart

bookbub.com/profile/lorhainne-eckhart

pinterest.com/lorhainneeckhart

Also by Lorhainne Eckhart

The Outsider Series

The Forgotten Child (Brad and Emily)
A Baby and a Wedding *(An Outsider Series Short)*
Fallen Hero (Andy, Jed, and Diana)
The Awakening (Andy and Laura)
Secrets (Jed and Diana)
Runaway (Andy and Laura)
Overdue *(An Outsider Series Short)*
The Unexpected Storm (Neil and Candy)
The Wedding (Neil and Candy)

The Friessens: A New Beginning

The Deadline (Andy and Laura)
The Price to Love (Neil and Candy)
A Different Kind of Love (Brad and Emily)
A Vow of Love, A Friessen Family Christmas

The Friessens

The Reunion
The Bloodline (Andy & Laura)
The Promise (Diana & Jed)
The Business Plan (Neil & Candy)
The Decision (Brad & Emily)
First Love (Katy)
Family First
Leave the Light On
In the Moment
In the Family
In the Silence

The Stalker
The O'Connell Family Christmas
The Girl Next Door
Broken Promises
The Gatekeeper
The Hunted

The McCabe Brothers

Don't Stop Me (Vic)
Don't Catch Me (Chase)
Don't Run From Me (Aaron)
Don't Hide From Me (Luc)
Don't Leave Me (Claudia)
Out of Time

A Billy Jo McCabe Mystery

Nothing As it Seems
Hiding in Plain Sight
The Cold Case
The Trap
Above the Law
The Stranger at the Door
The Children
The Last Stand
The Charity
The Sacrifice

The Street Fighter

Finding Home

The Wilde Brothers

The One (Joe and Margaret)
The Honeymoon, A Wilde Brothers Short
Friendly Fire (Logan and Julia)

Not Quite Married, A Wilde Brothers Short
A Matter of Trust (Ben and Carrie)
The Reckoning, A Wilde Brothers Christmas
Traded (Jake)
Unforgiven (Samuel)
The Holiday Bride

Married in Montana
His Promise
Love's Promise
A Promise of Forever

The Parker Sisters
Thrill of the Chase
The Dating Game
Play Hard to Get
What We Can't Have
Go Your Own Way
A June Wedding

Kate & Walker
One Night
Edge of Night
Last Night

Walk the Right Road Series
The Choice
Lost and Found
Merkaba
Bounty
Blown Away: The Final Chapter
He Came Back

The Saved Series

Lightning Source UK Ltd.
Milton Keynes UK
UKHW011134060323
418105UK00006B/852

9 781998 775491